New TOEIC Listening Script

*plug
v. 塞住、再宣傳
打廣告

→ He has been playing his new song on the radio.

苦幹: She plugged away with her math.
超認真唸數學

PART 1

煮水壺
n. 線、約束

1. (D) (A) The cord is twisted around the kettle.
電磁爐
(B) The induction cooker is plugged into the outlet.
電源插座 通路
(C) The man wants an outlet for his energy.
出口 (感情、精力)
精力需要發洩的出口
(D) A plug has been pulled out of the outlet.
插頭從插座裡拔出來

2. (C) (A) The house's upper windows are open.
*banner
n. 獲、旗幟
橫幅
(B) A banner is hanging from the ceiling. 天花板有布條垂下
(C) Chimneys rise above the roofs. 屋頂上有煙囪
(D) Men are climbing the ladder. 在爬梯子
/klaim/ climb

adj. 傑出的 This has been a banner year in sales. 銷售超好的一年

3. (D) (A) The windows are wide open. 窗戶大開
(B) The flower box shades the window.
(C) The trees are in front of the windows.
(D) The plants are growing in the window box.

工廠的產品有受到控管，怕有缺陷
stick to ① 堅持 ② 忠於
He is a man who sticks to his friends.
Everybody should stick to his post.

4. (D) (A) Some notes are stuck to the monitor.
adj. 有缺陷的
(B) The factory's output is monitored for defective items.
產量
down make, do
(C) The nurse is monitoring the patient's condition carefully. 護士仔細的監看病患的情況
(D) The patient is connected to the monitor. 病患和監控器連結在一起

*chase /e/ v. 追逐、驅逐 : She chased the children from the yard.

5. (B) (A) This is a cheesecake. * chew ①
(B) This is a chess tournament. /tʃu/ ① 深思熟慮
chase ①
(C) He likes chasing girls. He took my offer after chewing on it. 想過之後接受我
(D) He likes chewing gum.

→ I'll chew the problem over for a few days. 我掂了 的提議
幾天

6. (A) (A) The professor is giving a lecture.
n. 課 訓斥
(B) The dancers are performing on a stage. 上了一堂課
行人正穿越(C) The pedestrians are crossing the street. 罵了我一頓
馬路 (D) The salesman is signing a contract.
foot 人

教訓 Don't lecture me.
別對我說教

PART 2

這裡蠻暗的。   你介不介意我開燈

✱ make up

① 補足 We need $50 to make up the sum required.
需要50元來補足所需

7. (A) It's dark in here. Would you mind if I turned on a light?

(A) Suit yourself. 請自便

② 編造 The whole story is made up.
整個故事是虛構的

(B) Make up your mind. 請做出決定

(C) Bite the bullet. 硬著頭皮做 / 接受不愉快的事

紅
bite on granite 白費力氣.徒勞無益

bite one's tongue 強忍著不說出自己的想法

8. (B) Which one is your girlfriend?   右邊那位

(A) Up. 往上

→ When you are very angry, you had better bite your tongue so as not to say anything that would make you sorry.

(B) The one on the right.

(C) We're single.

別說出會讓自己後悔的話

為何維修人員會在這兒?

9. (A) Why are the maintenance guys here?

(A) To test the smoke alarms. 測試煙霧偵測器

(B) Once a week or so. 大約一周一次

(C) The short one is the brains of the operation. 較矮的那位是公司的腦
（重要人物）

那裡的天氣如何?

✱ temper ⓝ 脾氣. 冷靜

→ She has a sweet temper.
她脾氣溫和

10. (A) How's the weather there?

(A) Gorgeous. adj. 華麗的.豪華的

up stand (站在旁覺得聲許) adj. 迷信的

(B) Superstitious

→ She kept her husband in temper.
她讓丈夫保持冷靜

(C) Awkward. adj. 笨拙的.棘手的.不適合的
ɔ kwəd

Robert 脾氣不好嗎?

11. (C) Does Robert have a bad temper?

(A) Yes, the temperature went up to 30°C. 是的. 溫度高到30度

(B) No, I seldom lost my temper. 不.我很少失去脾氣(脾氣失控)

(C) Yes, he is so grumpy. adj. 脾氣暴躁的 ✱ temper ⓥ
/grʌmpɪ/

你打算待多久?

鍛鍊 Hardships tempered his will.
艱困使得鍛鍊了他的意志

12. (A) How long do you plan to stay?

(A) About two more days. 大約再兩天

(B) I arrived with my friends. 我和朋友一起到的

(C) We'll have to change our plans. 我們需要改變計劃

你和一個叫 Mulder 的代理人熟嗎?

13. (A) Are you familiar with an agent named Mr. Mulder?

(A) No, I've never heard of him. 不.我從來沒有聽過他 hear of 聽說過

(B) Yes, I need a travel agent. 是.我需要旅行社代辦員

adj.
(C) Yes, you and I are very similar. 對.你和我非常相像

熟知的.親手的 → she wrote in a familiar style. / Your face seems familiar.
慣親的   她用親切的筆調寫作   看上去很面熟

GO ON TO THE NEXT PAGE.

14. (C) Will you have time to visit the <u>factory</u>? 你有時間去拜訪工廠嗎？
    (A) Denmark.
    (B) We make them. 那些是我們做的
    (C) No, maybe next time. 不，也許下一次

make place / do
plant n. 植物 v. 種植 n. 工廠

15. (C) Do you come here often? 你常來這裡嗎？
    (A) Tomorrow. 明天
    (B) He's the owner. 他是老闆
    (C) No, this is my first time. 這是我第一次

21. advise v. advice n.
(v.) My doctor advised me to start taking a number of vitamins.
(n.) Could you give me some advice on how to learn English?

16. (B) Have you ever tried stinky tofu? 你有試過臭豆腐嗎？
    (A) Let's have something to eat. 我們來吃些東西吧
    (B) No. What does it taste like? 沒有，嚐起來如何
    (C) Yes. I have tried them all. 是的，我都試過了。(但問題只有一項物品) 所以不能 "them all"

17. (C) Do you have any sales experience? 你有任何銷售經驗嗎？
    (A) The class starts tomorrow. 這個班明天開始
    (B) Loveable. adj. 可愛的 = lovable = adorable What a lovable baby! ㅇㅂㅇ
    (C) No, I don't.

respond v. response n. → I'll respond to your email later.

18. (A) Where are you from? 你是哪裡人 ＊Where are you coming from? 你從哪裡來
    (A) I'm from central Pennsylvania. 我是賓夕法尼亞州中部人 /pɛnsɪlˈvenjə/
    (B) I know where you're coming from. 我知道你從哪裡來
    (C) I haven't seen him lately. 我最近沒有見到他
    → adv. 最近、近來、不久前

→ We're looking forward to your response.

19. (C) How long were you locked out of the house? 你被鎖在門外多時間？
    (A) The door was locked. 門被鎖起來了
    (B) I forgot my key. 忘記 key 了
    (C) About an hour. 大約一小時

Have you seen her lately?

20. (C) Didn't you go to <u>high school</u> with Marcy? 你不是跟 Marcy 一起上高中嗎? (9~12 年級)
    (A) I graduated in 2020. 我 2020 畢業
    (B) No, we went to high school together. 不，我們一起上高中
    (C) Yes, we were classmates. 是，我們是同學。

junior high senior high school 國中 高中
＊兄長 senior / 弟 junior

21. (B) How many orders did we receive? 我們收到過幾張訂單
    (A) Good night. Drive safely. 晚安，小心開車
    (B) Over three hundred. 超過 3 百
    (C) Advice is better to give than to receive. 給建議比收建議好，去掉 advice

It's better to give than receive 施比受更有福

→ New research by Wharton's Behavior Change for Good Initiative shows that while offering advice benefits the receiver, it also boosts the giver's self-confidence.

22. (C) What did you <u>think of</u> Irene? 你覺得 Irene 怎樣？ 27, seem
   (A) Think again, my friend. 思考清楚,我的朋友　　看起来好何.似乎
   (B) Her name is Irene. 我的名字是 Irene.
   (C) I thought she was very nice. 我覺得她很好　How does she seem today?
   她今天氣色如何？

你絕對猜不到我在商場看到了誰？　She seems very happy

23. (B) You'll never guess who I saw at the shopping mall!! with the new job.
   (A) What? 什麼？　＊breathe v. 呼吸.輕拂
   (B) Who? 誰？　/briðl/　The wind breathed over the lake.
   (C) How much? 多少錢？　He breathed a sign of relief.

你為何呼吸那麼大力？　發出如釋重負的嘆息聲

24. (A) Why are you <u>breathing</u> so hard?　＊breath n.氣
   (A) I ran all the way home. 我一路跑回家　/breθ/
   (B) I just woke up. 我剛起床　→ After all that running,
   (C) I need something to drink. 我需要一些喝的　he was short of breath.

你簽合約之前有先看過合約嗎？　跑步之後.他上氣不接下氣

25. (C) Did you read the contract before you signed it? 傷疤
   (A) What deep wound ever healed without a scar?
   (B) No, that's what babysitters are for. 那就是保姆的作用 ＋nanny (有執照)
   (C) Yes, I read it over twice. 有,我讀完兩次
   → wound /wund/ 傷口 heal 治療.痊癒 "沒有傷疤.深的傷口怎麼會好"
   (所以有傷疤也是合理的)

26. (C) You were born in Atlanta, weren't you? 要點觀看待.面對
   (A) It's about an hour from Macon. 從 Macon大約
   (B) I was there yesterday. 我昨天在那兒　一小時　你是亞特蘭大出生的.是嗎？
   (C) Yes, I was. 我是。

你派對有很多賓客嗎？　＊wound
　　　　　　　　　　　　☑傷害: The shot wounded her left arm.
27. (A) Were there many guests at your party?　子彈打傷了左臂
   (A) About fifty. 大約50人
   (B) They seemed to be happy. 他們好像很開心　回傷害.創傷
   (C) Not more than twenty dollars. 不超過20元　That was a wound to the
　　　　　　　　　　　　　　　　　　　　　　kid's pride.

你的襯衫怎麼了？

28. (C) What happened to your shirt? stripe n.條紋 <口>類型.特點
   (A) Stripes aren't my style. /straɪp/　He is a politician of
   (B) It fits very well. 非常合身　the worst stripe. 最不入流的
   (C) I <u>spilled</u> paint on it. 我把漆潑到上面 ＊spill v. 溢出　政客
都覺得你的演講(演出.呈現)如何？　洩露: Spill out the information

29. (B) How did the client react to your presentation? 跌下: The rider spilt in dust.
   (A) I voted for Eisenhower twice. 我投給艾兩次　跌落在地
   (B) They seemed to be very impressed. 他們看起來印象深刻
   (C) I <u>looked</u> for their reactions. 我期待他們的反應

尋找.期待

GO ON TO THE NEXT PAGE.

30. (B) Did you see Norman at the party? 你在派隊有看到 Norman 嗎?
    (A) It was a party. ＊rate
    (B) Yes, he was there. n. 比例·率·費用·等級
    (C) Only Norman.   She gave her children a first-rate education.

是誰負責訂辦公室用品? v. 評估 How do you rate our chances of success?

31. (A) Who is in charge of ordering the office supplies? 被評價 The hotel doesn't rate
    (A) Check with the secretary. 和秘書確認一下   five stars at all.
    (B) There is a stapler on my desk. 我桌上有個釘書機   = worried
    (C) Friday night.   staple 釘書針   = fearful = troubled

＊anxious
/ˈæŋkʃəs/ adj. 焦慮的 = uneasy = concerned

PART 3
渴望的 = We are anxious for your safe
掛念的: I am anxious about   return.
→ desirous = Keen   her safety.

Questions 32 through 34 *refer to the following conversation.*   → carefree
他們宣佈了寫作比賽的得獎者了嗎?   insouciant
M : Have they announced the winners of the writing contest? /ɪnˈsuːsɪənt/ 漠不經心的
W : Not yet. I heard it won't be until after lunch. (announced)   不在乎的
還沒! 我聽說不到午餐後不會宣佈   有很多參賽者
M : You must be very anxious. 你一定非常焦慮 和有才華的競爭者
W : Well, there were so many contestants and talented competitors. I'm not sure how I rate
   against them, so I haven't got my hopes up, I can tell you that. 我不確定我如何和他們比較
說話者在等什麼?   所以我不敢抱太大希望
32. (B) What are the speakers waiting for?   我可以老實跟你說.
    (A) To enter a contest. 參加比賽
    (B) To hear the results of a contest. 聽比賽的結果 ＊contestant
    (C) To meet the winner of the contest. 和比賽得主見面 challenger 人
    (D) To read the entries in the contest. 閱讀比賽的日誌·記錄 participant
對於女生所指何者為真?   entrant
33. (A) What is implied about the woman? imply   racer
    (A) She entered the contest. 參加比賽   player
    (B) She works in publishing. 在出版業工作
    (C) She was the favorite to win the contest. 他最有可能贏得比賽
    (D) She has a changeable temperament. 他有易變的性格
    → 氣質·性格·性情
34. (D) How does the woman feel?   He has a romantic temperament.
    (A) Confident. adj. 自信的·大膽的   有浪漫的性格
    (B) Angry.
    (C) Bored.
    (D) Doubtful. ① 懷疑的 ② 不明確的 The future looks very doubtful.

Questions 35 through 37 refer to the following conversation.

這裡是紀錄部門嗎?

W : Is this the Department of Records?

這裡是檔案記錄中心. 你實際上是要找什麼?

M : This is the Archives and Records Center. What exactly are you looking for?

/ˈɑrkaɪv/ n. 檔案. 文件. 記錄   , n. 法令. 命令

W : I need a certified copy of my name change decree. 我需要我改名的正式文件證明

~adj. 認證的. 被證明的

M : OK, well, that would be on the second floor. Room 212. They handle certifications. Do you
   have your case number? 那會在2樓(實際是3樓)國外一樓叫 ground floor

他們處理證照文件. 你有檔案編號嗎?

W : No, the judge said I wouldn't need it. The information sheet he gave me says to come here,
   to Room 112, with a valid driver's license, pay the fee, and that's it.

但是裁決者(評判人)說我不需要檔案號. 資訊單只說來這裡到112室

35. (B) Where are the speakers?
          他給我的
   (A) In a public park. 公園
   (B) In a government building. 政府大樓   帶著有效的駕照. 付錢. 就可以了
   (C) In a sporting arena. 運動館場   *valid adj. 合法的. 有效的
   (D) In a whirlwind romance.

   /ˈhwɝl, wɪnd/ n. 旋風 → 閃愛. 閃婚. 很快陷入愛河

36. (A) What does the woman want?
   (A) A document. 文件   The ticket is valid for a month.
complain (B) To file a complaint. 申訴客訴   這票一個月內有效
v.抱怨 (C) A haircut. 剪頭髮
   (D) To appear in court. 出庭   This is a valid contract.
                                   有效的合約
                      *strictly
37. (C) What will the woman most likely do next? 僅. 完全地
   (A) Call the judge. → The car park is strictly for the use of
   (B) Stay in Room 112.   residence.
   (C) Go to Room 212.   僅供居民使用
   (D) Pay the fee.   → I think, strictly speaking, you're wrong here.

*hold someone in check 不讓某人變得太有權. please hold your voice in check 壓低

Questions 38 through 40 refer to the following conversation.

感謝大家的認真工作. Maria   庭院看起來超棒   草叢修整一下彎好的   嗓門

M : Thanks for all your hard work, Maria. The yard looks fantastic, and it's nice to have the
   bushes trimmed. However, I was wondering if you could do me a small favor.

W : I'll try, sir. 可是. 我在想你是否可以幫我個小忙

你可以先留著這張支票到周四再兑   因為我到周四才有薪水. 而我不想要

M : Could you please hold this check until Thursday? I don't get paid until then, and I don't 跳票
   want it to bounce. 跳票 → 這會是個問題. 其實咧. 我通常不接受個人支票

W : That's going to be a problem, sir. You see, I don't usually accept personal checks for my
   work. Strictly cash. But I'll tell you what. How about if I come back on Saturday and you
   can pay me then? 只收現金. 但我跟你說. 不如我周六回來. 你到時再付錢給我

GO ON TO THE NEXT PAGE. ➡

M : OK, that's a fair deal. Thanks for understanding. <u>Come by</u> Saturday morning and I'll have the cash ready for you. 好的. 公平的交易. 謝謝你的體諒

周六早上過來. 然後我會把現金準備好給你

38. (B) What position does Maria hold? Maria是擔任什麼職位

    (A) Janitor. n. 看門人. 看屋. 監工工人 　*come by ① 沒費力走過去
    (B) Gardener. 園藝工人　　　　　He has just come by.
    (C) Housemaid. 女佣　　②得到. 獲得. How did you come by
    (D) Mechanic. ㄇㄎ n. 技工. 修理工　接近　this tool? 你怎麼得到這項の

39. (B) What problem does the man have? 這個男的有什麼問題

*trim　(A) His <u>bushes</u> need to be <u>trimmed</u>. 灌木叢需要修整　* I am beat.
v.修剪　(B) He can't pay Maria until Thursday. 不到周四無法付她錢　I am bushed.
削減　(C) He isn't happy with Maria's service. 他對服務不滿意　好累~
修改　(D) He <u>ran out of</u> personal checks. 個人支票用完了
    run out of 用完

40. (D) What will happen on Saturday? 周六會發生什麼事?　*plant
adj.　(A) Maria will plant more flowers. 種更多的花　n. 植物 v. 種植
鬢角的　(B) The man will write a personal check. 寫張個人支票　n. 工廠
端正的　(C) The man will go to the bank. 去銀行　→ plant a bomb 安置炸彈
    (D) Maria will get paid. 得到錢　→ plant biology 植物學
She always looks neat and trim. 看起来很端正剖整　→ plant food 肥料

Questions 41through 43 refer to the following conversation.
你去Boston會議的飛機票訂好了嗎? → plant culture 作物栽培
W : Hey, Brian. Have you booked your flight to the conference in Boston yet?

M : Not yet, Louise. I haven't decided if I should fly on Tuesday evening or Wednesday morning. 還沒. 我還沒決定 周二晚上 or 周三早上飛

我是搭周二晚飛機　　　　　我想在周三會議前安置好並休息一下
W : I'm on the Tuesday evening flight. I want to get settled in the hotel and rest a little bit before the conference begins on Wednesday. 好主意. 也許我也會那麼做

M : That's a good idea. Maybe I'll do the same.
我建議你早點打給航空公司, 總比來不及好.　我今天早上訂我的票時
W : I suggest you call the airline <u>sooner rather than later</u>. When I booked my ticket this morning, the agent told me the flight was almost sold out. 專員跟我說機票幾乎賣光了

* sooner or later 遲早　* drive an arguement home
41. (C) Why are the speakers traveling to Boston?　把論點講透
    (A) To settle an argument. 安撫一場爭論
    (B) To save money. 存錢　tear sb's argument to rags
    (C) To attend a conference. 參加會議　把某人論點駁得體無完膚
    (D) To sell products. 賣商品
*rather than 而不是　　　　rag n. 惡作劇. 喧鬧
These shoes are comfortable rather than　Some kids ragged him about his
這些鞋子很舒服而不是漂亮　pretty.　big nose. 嘲笑他的大鼻子

52

42. (C) When does Louise's flight leave for Boston?
    (A) Yesterday. *38. trim*
    (B) Today. *修剪整理.布置 The children are trimming up*
    (C) Tuesday evening. *a Christmas tree.*
    (D) Wednesday morning. *調整(使船和)平穩: The sailors trimmed*
    the boat.

43. (A) What does the woman suggest?
    (A) Call the airline soon. *(n) 狀況.情形: Is our team in trim for the game?*
    (B) Wait until Wednesday. *我們隊準備好去比賽了嗎?*
    (C) Use a different airline. *整齊.潔: The room is in good trim.*
    (D) Skip the conference. *修剪整: The hedge needs a trim. 籬笆需要修整*

Questions 44 through 46 *refer to the following conversation with three speakers.*

你一定會喜歡這個地方   每樣都好吃而且份量很大方   份量
W1: You're going to love this place. Everything is delicious and the portions are very generous.

M : Mm. A cheeseburger would sure hit the spot. How about you, Ann?
    起司漢堡正合我意   hit the high spots 達到高水準.觸到要點
W2: I'd like a bowl of soup and a salad. *我要一碗湯和沙拉*

W1: The chef's salad is delicious but it's very big. I'm not sure I could eat anything else with
    that. *主廚沙拉好吃但是很大份. 我不確定吃了沙拉後我能吃下其他東西*
    我又要薯條搭配我的漢堡   你們為何不分食一個大沙拉
M : Well, I just want fries with my burger. Hey, why don't you two split a big salad and each
    order something else to go with it? *然後再各自點東西搭配*

W2: Great idea!
    *好的. 然後我會點個火腿三明治給自己   *satisfy ㄙㄟㄊ虹*
W1: Yeah, I'll do that, and I'll order a ham sandwich for myself.
    →使滿意
                                                          The answer won't satisfy her.
44. (D) What do the women agree to do?
    (A) Go to another restaurant. *去別的餐廳* *→滿足(足慾)*
    (B) Order soup and salad. *湯和沙拉* *Her remarks satisfied his*
    (C) Pay for the man's lunch. *幫男生付午餐錢* *doubts.*
    (D) Share a large salad. *分享更大的沙拉* *→償還(債務),履行(義務)*

                                                          Both sides strove to
45. (B) What does the man mean when he says "hit the spot"? *satisfy the*
    (A) It is a great spot to eat. *這是很適合吃東西的地方* *contract.*
    (B) A burger would satisfy him. *一個漢堡能滿足他*
    (C) He would like to get his food quickly. *想快點拿到食物*
    (D) The woman is correct about the salad. *對於沙拉是正確的*

＊Are you satisfied that he is telling the truth?
你確信他在說真話嗎?   打網球是他最大樂趣之一 *双方都努力履行契約*
→ satisfaction n.滿意.滿足.稱心.樂事. Playing tennis is one of his greatest satisfactions.
ㄙㄟㄊ

GO ON TO THE NEXT PAGE.

46. (A) Look at the graphic. How much will the man pay for his food?
　　(A) $7.50.
　　(B) $8.00.
　　(C) $11.50.
　　(D) $15.50.

Nellie's Diner
Lunch Menu

Salads
Chef's Salad　$8　　　　　Taco Salad　$8

Soups
Tomato　　　　　　　　　　cup $2
Soup of the Day　　　　　　bowl $5

Sandwiches — served with fries or potato chips
Roast beef, Chicken or Ham　　　　$7
Vegetable　　　　　　　　　　$6

Burgers — served with fries or potato chips
Hamburger　　　　　　　　　　$7
Cheeseburger　　　　　　　　　$7.50
Bacon Cheeseburger　　　　　　$8

Questions 47 through 49 refer to the following conversation.

M : Have you finished updating the files I gave you?

W : Yes, they're on your desk.

M : How about the missing purchasing receipts? Were you able to locate them?

W : I sure was. I sent them up to accounting as per your instructions.

M : Well done. Why don't you take the rest of the day off?

47. (C) Who are the speakers?
　　(A) Doctor and patient.
　　(B) Student and teacher.
　　(C) Supervisor and employee.
　　(D) Brother and sister.

48. (B) What did the woman do with the updated files?
   (A) She gave them to the secretary.
   (B) She put them on the man's desk.
   (C) She left them at home.
   (D) Nothing.

49. (C) What did the woman do with the purchasing receipts?
   (A) She lost them.
   (B) She paid them.
   (C) She sent them to the accounting department.
   (D) She left them on the man's desk.

Questions 50 through 52 refer to the following conversation.

M : Hi, Rachel. Mr. Edwin sent me to pick up the employee time cards. Have you received all of them?

W : Hi, Kenny. Almost. I'm still waiting on a few from the second shift. Those guys don't punch out until midnight. Mr. Edwin knows that.

M : Actually, I think he forgot. We've got our hands full upstairs, you know, processing all the holiday orders.

W : I understand, Kenny. Tell Mr. Edwin I'll run the time cards up to his office first thing in the morning.

50. (D) What does Kenny want?
   (A) A job on the second shift.
   (B) To punch out at midnight.
   (C) To place a holiday order.
   (D) The employee time cards.

51. (B) What does Rachel say?
   (A) She is working the second shift.
   (B) She doesn't have all the time cards yet.
   (C) She told Mr. Edwin about the holiday.
   (D) She doesn't understand the problem.

52. (A) What will Rachel do tomorrow?
   (A) Bring the time cards to Mr. Edwin.
   (B) Call Kenny to come and get the time cards.
   (C) Return the time cards to the employees.
   (D) Place her holiday orders.

GO ON TO THE NEXT PAGE.

55

我們要看哪部電影?
M1: So which movie do we want to see?

n.喜劇
W : How about Love's All That? I hear it's a great comedy.

噢噢 拜拖 不要再看浪漫喜劇了   a⊃ェ ①我寧願看最後的戰役
M2: Ugh. Please, not another romantic comedy. I'd rather see The Final Battle.

W : You know I hate war movies. How about the new Bond movie as a compromise?

你知道我不喜歡戰爭電影. 新的007電影做為一個折衷(妥協)好嗎?
M1: I'll go along with that, but we have to go to the early show. I need to be home by nine.

W : Fine with me.   我同意   但我們要看早一點的   我9:00前要到家

M2: Me, too!

her views
you on that point   * compromise
her wishes

53. (B) What kind of movies does the woman like? →達成妥協
恐怖小說 (A) Thrillers.   I hope we shall come to a
(電影)   (B) Romantic comedies.   compromise.
(驚悚然的) (C) Action movies.   →危急 She did it without
         (D) Horror movies.   compromise of her reputation.
              (鬼怪)恐怖電影

54. (D) Look at the graphic. What time will the speakers see a movie?
escape   (A) 9:00.   →放棄 He refused to compromise
㈣逃跑   (B) 6:00.   his principles.
         (C) 8:45.
He made (D) 6:20. *escape ⓥ逃跑,避免 He traveled extensively to
his escape   escape from boredom.
in disguise.

CINEPARK THEATER			
The Great Escape	6:15	8:20	10:45
Bond Returns Again	6:20	8:45	11:00
Love's All That	6:00	8:00	10:00
Harry Houdini	7:30	10:30	
The Final Battle	7:00	9:00	11:00

他偽裝後逃走了
解悶
She reads
detective
stories as

流出.漏出
Gas is escaping from the
                    pipe.
*taste
味覺.口味,愛好
She has a taste for music.

an escape. 她看偵探小說解悶
55. (A) Why does the woman suggest a compromise? 為何要提出折衷方案
            (A) She and the man have different tastes in movies. 對電影有不同品味
* rather (B) She would like to pay for the movie tickets. 想付電影票錢
①.排名.顏 (C) She promised that she would see the Bond movie. 答應要看007
有異見   (D) The war movie is too long. 戰爭電影太長

→ I'm feeling rather sleepy.   ③和 or 更用·更確切的說
⊙ would rather 寧可.寧願   He left late last night, or rather early
→ He would rather play than work.   this morning.
→ I'd rather you know that now, than afterwards.

在某以後了解你知道.不如現在讓你知道

W : Hi, Tom. How's it going?

M : Terrible, Sue. I just lost my job! 我剛沒了工作

W : Oh, that is terrible. What happened? 好可怕,真糟糕 發生什麼事

M : Apparently, the company is downsizing. A bunch of us got laid off last week.
很明顯地,公司正在縮編 我們好多人上周被辭退了

* lay off
解雇,停止使用,別搔擾

Lay him off!
Lay me off, can't you?

56. (D) Who are the speakers?
    (A) Strangers. 陌生人
    (B) Co-workers. 同事
    (C) Employer and employee.
    (D) Friends.

* stretch
v. 伸直,伸出
She stretched out her hand
for the dictionary.

57. (B) What happened to the man?
    (A) He lost his wallet. 錢包丟了
    (B) He lost his job. 工作丟了
    (C) He lost his house keys.
    (D) He lost his dog.

展開,鋪開
The eagle stretches its wings.
延續,連綿
The desert stretches for thousand
of miles.

58. (B) What does the man imply?
    (A) His former employer is making a lot of money. 前老闆賺了很多錢
    (B) Some of his co-workers lost their jobs, too.
    (C) He should have paid the taxi driver. 應該要付錢給司機
    (D) His manager is finding new jobs. 經理在找新工作

* first come first served
先來先得
serve one's interest
為一的利益服務
serve one's sentence
服刑,生牢

* serving
一份
a serving
of vegetables / It's enough for four servings. 足夠四個人吃

讓我重複一下你的訂單 你要兩箱可樂 一箱低卡一箱正常
W : All right, Mr. Swift. Let me repeat your order. You want two cases of Coke—one diet and
one regular; 50 one-serving bags of potato chips—original flavor; and 50 ham and cheese
sandwiches. Is that correct? 50袋一次性包裝的薯片(原味) / 50個火腿起司三明治

M : Yes, it is. And can I expect that to arrive before noon? It's for attendees of our seminar.
是的我可以期望是中午前到嗎? 是為了研討會的參加者訂的 就算我們全部人員都做三

W : That's going to be somewhat of a stretch, Mr. Swift. Even though I've got my whole crew on 明
the sandwiches, we're looking at 12:30—at the earliest. Perhaps you could move the lunch 治
period back to 1:00, just to be safe? 我們也希望 12=30(最早) 或者你可以把午餐時間移到
有點勉強   1:00,比較保險?

M : Well, I know this is a last-minute order. Someone forgot to take care of it yesterday—that's
not your fault. I suppose there's nothing to do but move the lunch period back to 1:00.
我知道這是個緊急訂單,有人昨天忘記下單,不是你的錯,我想除了移到1:00之外也無他法

W : Tell you what—just to ease a bit of your pain, how about if I throw in an extra 50 chocolate
chip cookies, on the house? 跟你說,為了減輕一點你的痛苦(麻煩)
我多給你50個巧克力脆片餅乾、店家請.如何?

GO ON TO THE NEXT PAGE.

59. (A) What is the relationship between the speakers? * suppose
     (A) Salesperson and customer. 銷售員和客人 (V.) 猜想，以為
     (B) Teacher and student. → I suppose he is still in town.
     (C) Husband and wife. → You are not supposed to take the books out of the room. 不應該
     (D) Boss and employee.

custom 習俗
Customs 海關

60. (A) What is the man's problem? → 祈使語氣 Suppose we set out at six. 我們6點出發吧！
*appointment (A) The order wasn't placed yesterday. 昨天沒有下訂單
     (B) Too many people have attended the seminar. 太多人參加研討會
約會，會面 (C) He doesn't have enough money to pay the bill. 沒有足夠的錢付帳單
任命，職位 (D) He is late for an appointment. 約會要遲到了

61. (C) What does the woman suggest? 女生所指何者為真
     (A) Order more soda.
I accepted (B) Choose a different sandwich. 選不一樣的三明治
the appointment (C) Move the lunch period.
as chairman. (D) Cancel the seminar.
我同意擔任主席一職

Insomnia 失眠

*dormant
adj. 睡著的、靜止的、休眠的 dormant volcano 休
active 活
extinct 死

Questions 62 through 64 refer to the following conversation with three speakers.

dormitive 安眠藥
sleeping pills tablets

W1: Help! I can't get this online registration to work! 幫我，這線上註冊動不了
M : Maybe the course is already full. 可能課程已經滿了
W2: Yeah, I had that problem with one of my classes. 對，我其中一堂課也有這個問題
W1: Oh, no! I really need this class! And this is the only section that fits my schedule. 我真的需要這個課，而且這是唯一符合我行程表的課
M : Wait, I see the problem. You missed one of the boxes. 等，我發現問題了，那一格你沒填
W2: Gary's right. See there? You need to fill that in. Then click submit. 你要把項填這格，然後按繳交

* submit
under / send

62. (D) What is the woman trying to do?
submit (A) Submit a paper. 繳交報告
繳交，提交 (B) Register for a room in the dormitory. 註冊宿舍裡的一間房 = (dorm)
屈從，忍受 (C) Find out what time her class starts. 找出她課程何時開始
     (D) Enroll in a course. 註冊課程
under / send
She refused to submit to his control.
*fit v. 合身，適合

63. (B) What does Gary suggest? 課程不符合她的行程 → We must fit the action to the word.
     (A) The class will not (fit) her schedule. 說一致
We'll submit (B) The class might be full. 課可能滿了
ourselves (C) The woman is not good at using computers. 不太會使用電腦
to the (D) The online registration system has many problems. 線上註冊系統有許多問題
court's judgement. 我們將哺從法庭的裁決

便繳交，便要到） The metal was submitted to analysis. 這錢屋受到分析

58

64. (D) Look at the graphic. Why was the woman unsuccessful?

*fill in
項意

fill in for
臨時代替

My partner
is on holiday
this week
so I'm
filling in for
him.

*fill out
①填寫表格
He has to fill the form out.
②發胖 Her cheeks began to fill out.

(A) She did not click SUBMIT.
(B) She did not write her home address.
(C) She did not fill in her e-mail address.
(D) She did not fill in her phone number.

不成功 = adj.

success n. 成功.成就.勝利)
→ to meet with success
→ wish you every success
祝嬴到成功
→ to make a success of sth.
把某事做成功

*successful
adj. 成功的.圓滿的
*successfully
adv. 順利地.成功地.

Online Registration

Name*	Ann Temple
Student number*	43981286
E-mail address	
Phone number*	
Address	Room 207 Shaw Dormitory
Course number*	A402
Section number*	12

* indicates required field 表示(指出)
沙項區塊心 SUBMIT

⑤出(錢) How much did she
come down with?
她出了多少錢
→The girl has come down with flu.
①得~病.染上~病

Questions 65 through 67 refer to the following conversation.

我喉嚨痛   我覺得我可能染上什麼病 come down with
M : My throat hurts. I think I may be coming down with something.

還沒 我有約明天早上
W : Have you been to see a doctor? 你有去看醫生嗎?

M : Not yet. I have an appointment for tomorrow morning.

W : Good. It's always better to nip these things in the bud. 4③.把這些事死在尚未發芽時
v.夾.掐.摘   n.芽   就好提掉 免4③事
                              v.發芽 (防患未然.發生前先扼殺)
65. (A) What is the man's problem?
                              → The apple trees are budding.
(A) He might be getting sick.
(B) He needs a ride home. 需要有人
(C) He wants to be free.   載回家 Do you need a ride? ✓
(D) He lost his job.   Let me bring you home. ✗

66. (D) What will the man do tomorrow morning?
(A) Go to work. *come down ①倒塌 The ceiling came down suddenly.
(B) Go to class. ② 流傳下來 The story has come down from time
(C) Take a vacation.   immemorial. 遠古流傳至今
(D) See a doctor.   遠古的.遠古的
③價格.溫度降低.下降   ﾆ汽油降格在下降 ④失勢 He had come down in the
The price of petrol is coming down.   world.
                                  淪到

GO ON TO THE NEXT PAGE.

67. (A)　What does the woman say?

　　赞许　(A)　She approves of the man's decision. 她同意男主的決定
　　批準　(B)　She does not approve of the man's decision. 不同意
　　贊成　(C)　She wants to go along with the man. 她和他贊同. 意見相同
　　　　　(D)　She does not believe the man has a problem. 她不覺得男主有問題

→Her father will never approve of her marriage to Tom.

Questions 68 through 70 refer to the following conversation.

你想見我嗎?　　　　　sit down　　　　have a seat next to me
M : Hi, Katrina. You wanted to see me?

W : Yes, Otis. Please, have a seat. 是的. 請坐　please be seated

都OK嗎?　我覺得有些奇怪　你以前從來都沒有叫我來你辦公室過
M : Is everything OK? I feel kind of strange. You've never asked me to sit in your office before.

　Am I getting fired? 我要被炒了嗎?→ 你做得很好. 對公司來說也是很好的資產

W : Well, you see, Otis. You're doing a fantastic job and I think you're a great asset to this
company. Fired is not a word I like to use. No... how shall I put this? We are offering you
a temporary unpaid vacation, that is, until business picks up and we can bring you back
onboard. 我不想用"炒了"這個詞. 嗯. 該怎麼說呢? 我們提供你個暫時
adj.臨時的　　　　　　　　　　　　無薪假期. 也就是
68. (D)　What does Katrina imply to Otis?
暫時的　(A)　He is a lazy employee. 懶員工　　放到公司有起色. 再招你回來
　　　　　(B)　He should have been fired a long time ago. 很久之前就該被炒
a temporary (C)　He will find another job quickly. 很快可以找到其他工作
　Job　　(D)　He may have an opportunity to get his job back. 可能有機會再次得回

69. (C)　Who are the speakers?　　＊asset n. 財產. 資產. 寶貴的人才　工作
n.臨時工　(A)　Doctor and patient.　　　　　　　　　　　有益的品質. 有利條件
she works　(B)　Student and teacher. → Good health is a great asset.
in the office (C)　Supervisor and employee. =accounts, wealth, resources
as a temporary. (D)　Brother and sister.　　property, funds, goods, capital,

70. (B)　What does Otis suspect? v. 懷疑. 猜想　→ The tiger suspected
　　　　　(A)　He's about to be promoted. 差不多要升官了　danger and ran away.
＊promote (B)　He's about to be fired.　　　　　→ I suspect they'll come.
　　　　　(C)　He's about to get a raise. 差不多要加薪了　　我想他們會來的
Ⓥ　　　(D)　He's about to take a vacation. 差不多要放假了
①晉升 ②升級　　　　　　　　　　　　　　→The police suspected
Pupils who pass the test will be promoted to the　that Tom did it.
next higher grade. 通過考試的學生會升到高一个年級
③促進.引起 : The Prime Minister's visit will promote the cooperation between the
　　　　　　　　　　　　　　　　　　　　　two countries.
④發起.創立 = Several bankers promoted the new company.
⑤宣传.推銷 = Your job is to promote the new product.

PART 4

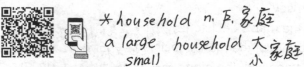

*household n. 戶. 家庭
a large household 大家庭
small 小家庭

Questions 71 through 73 *refer to the following news report.*

動50人受傷、271,400戶人家停電。在颱風襲了日本沖繩島之後

At least 50 people were injured and 271,400 households were left without power after

strike→struck→struck 災難官方過了這麼說的

Typhoon Jelawat struck Okinawa island of Japan, disaster officials there said Saturday.

當暴風對著日本島呱呱叫時 (狂風大雨)   3個人在九洲最南端受傷

As the storm roared toward other Japanese islands, three people were injured in the

/kju.su/   鹿兒島的災難管理辦公室說的

southernmost part of Kyushu, the Disaster Management Office of the Kagoshima

縣立的   縣府 颱風預計會到 aɪə
prefecture government said. The typhoon is expected to strike the Japanese mainland

prefecture n.縣 日本本島在周日的時候。最近幾周襲擊這區域的風呀風, Jelawat

on Sunday. The latest typhoon to hit the region in recent weeks, Jelawat is a "very

非常強勁. 最大持續風速靠近中心的風速每小時1000哩

strong" storm with maximum sustained winds near the center of just over 100 miles per

日本氣象中心說   NASA報告說這個氣旋

hour, the Japan Meteorological Agency said. A NASA advisory said the cyclone was

可以和了3級龍捲風相比   這個氣旋失去了些力度並且會持續

comparable to a category 3 hurricane. The cyclone has lost some of its might and

減弱   在靠近比較冷的水之後

should continue weakening after moving into colder waters, said CNN meteorologist

Karen Maginnis. Wind troughs out of China could divert Jelawat away from land and

into the open Pacific Ocean. /trɔf/ → 從大陸來的風槽. 會將Jelawat轉向
轉移日本土地. 到開闊的太平洋

71. (D) What is the speaker mainly discussing?   *trough n. 飼料槽. 飲水槽
娛樂   (A) Entertainment.
地理學   (B) Geography. earth writing   *meteorology n. 氣象學   *divert
經濟   (C) Economics.   air   v. 轉向. 轉移
天氣   (D) Weather.   meteorological adj. 氣象的

72. (B) What happened in Okinawa?   *advisor n. 顧問
    (A) It was struck by a tornado.   advisory n. 報告. 公告 adj. 顧問的
*injure   (B) At least 50 people were injured.   She wrote him an   ← 勸告的
/'ɪndʒər/   (C) Only three people were injured.   advisory letter.
傷害. 損壞 (D) Five people were killed.

*
electricity pylon 塔
73. (D) What did NOT happen in Japan?   electric   meter 計
失去電力   (A) Many homes lost electricity.   adj. 電的   bill 單
    (B) There were strong winds.   supply 供應
    (C) People were injured.   令人震驚的. 極其強烈的
政府宣布 (D) The government declared an emergency.   His speech had an electric
緊急情況   declare v.宣布. 聲明   on the audience. 這演講令觀眾
震驚不已

GO ON TO THE NEXT PAGE.

Good afternoon. As you know, my name is Nan Peck, and I'm pleased to talk with you about a topic that is near and dear to my head and my heart: listening skills. Your president tells me that this is important to you as well. Let me ask you this: On a scale of 1 to 10, how would you rate yourself as a listener? Most U.S. adults would rate themselves a 7.5. Unfortunately, according to the National Communication Association, if you're like most adults, you listen with just 25% efficiency! If you're like me, you realize that there is more to listening than meets the ear. If you're like me, you know that it's in your best interests to improve your listening skills. I've been studying listening and training people to improve their listening skills for more than 20 years. I spent 14 years training listeners for a suicide hotline and other professionals who recognize the importance of good listening. For the next thirty minutes, I'd like to share with you the five important listening <u>considerations</u> that I believe will help you get along better with your family and friends, and your colleagues. With the hope that you'll be actively listening to me, I invite you to stop me at any time and to ask me for <u>clarification</u>. I promise to listen to you, too.

74. (B) Who is the speaker?

(A) An expert on statistics.

(B) An expert on communication.

(C) An expert on corporate management.

(D) An expert on body language.

75. (A) What will the speaker talk about?

(A) Listening skills.

(B) Speaking skills.

(C) Study habits.

(D) Management styles.

76. (D) When can the audience ask questions?

(A) At the end of the speech.

(B) Before the speech begins.

(C) 30 minutes later.

(D) Any time.

OK, Bulls fans! Can I have your attention, please? We're about to announce the winner of tonight's Lucky Winner drawing. If your seat number is called, you'll win a fantastic prize package consisting of a Chicago Bulls team jacket, an autographed Derrick Rose poster, a $50 gift certificate to Big Al's Restaurant, and two tickets to an upcoming Bulls game. OK, get your tickets out. Tonight's lucky winner is sitting in... section 2, row 12, and seat... 23! Do we have a winner? Yes! There he is on the big screen. OK, great! So listen, buddy, to claim your prize, bring your ticket to the fan information booth adjacent to tunnel 28 before the end of the game. The rest of you, remember to keep your ticket stub from tonight's game. It entitles you to $5 off a regular wash and wax at any Pink Panda Car Wash location.

77. (A) Where is this announcement being made?

    (A) At a sports stadium.

    (B) In an airport.

    (C) In a restaurant.

    (D) At a public auction.

78. (A) What is the speaker offering?

    (A) A prize package.

    (B) An internship.

    (C) An autographed basketball.

    (D) A chance to play for the Bulls.

79. (D) Which of the following is NOT mentioned by the speaker?

    (A) Big Al's Restaurant.

    (B) Derrick Rose.

    (C) Pink Panda Car Wash.

    (D) The name of the winner.

GO ON TO THE NEXT PAGE.

Questions 80 through 82 *refer to the following traffic report.*

This is Anna Stasha with your KKP-FM traffic and weather on the ones. It's still early, folks, but so far so good out on the roads this morning, with no major delays to report. You're looking at standard commute times all over the tri-county area. However, starting tomorrow, the department of transportation will close the two left lanes of I-45 between Fuller Road and the Franken Freeway, in both directions. No word on what's going on there. Just avoid it if possible. Today's weather is as pleasant and predictable as today's traffic report, with clear skies and temps in the upper 70s, with maybe a slight breeze off the lake. Tonight, clear skies, lows in the mid-to-upper 60s. Tomorrow and the rest of the week look good, with no major storm fronts headed our way. Visit KKP's website for up-to-date traffic and weather conditions. This segment of KKP's traffic and weather was brought to you by State Farm Insurance. Like a good neighbor, State Farm is there. I'm Anna Stasha and now back to Rick and Dick's Morning Zoo.

80. (A) When was this report made?
   (A) In the early morning.
   (B) In the afternoon.
   (C) At noon.
   (D) In the evening.

81. (B) What will happen tomorrow?
   (A) It will rain.
   (B) Lane closures on I-45.
   (C) A slight breeze off the lake.
   (D) A parade on Fuller Road.

82. (A) Where would this report be heard?
   (A) On the radio.
   (B) In a newspaper.
   (C) On the Internet.
   (D) On the voice mail system.

64

我知道你說過要去公平交易商店在Polk市

Hi, Claire, it's David. Listen, I know you said you want to go to the Honest Traders

但是我們需要超級早起才能去

store in Polk City tomorrow, but we'd have to get up awfully early to do that. You know

你知道我一點前需要回來對吧. 我覺得最好9or10點離開

I need to be back by one, right? I think it would be better to leave around nine or ten.

在Freeport有另一個交易商店   我知道旅程較久

There's another Honest Traders in Freeport. I know it's a longer trip, but we'd still have

但我們仍有時間逛   而且看起來整天的巴士也比較頻繁 (車次多班)

plenty of time to shop. It also seems like the buses run more regularly throughout the

所以回程較不會有問題

day, so we'd have no trouble getting back. Give me a call back and let me know what

you think.

✻farther 程度上的更遠、進一步的. 更深層的

(adv) Do you need further help?

83. (D) What does David suggest?   (adv) We'll help you further.

早點出發 (A) Leaving early for Honest Traders.

13:00後再去 (B) Going to Honest Traders after one o'clock.   而且. The house is not big enough

for us; and further,

晚點出發 (C) Leaving for Polk City later in the day.   it is too far from the town.

去另外一個地方 (D) Going to a different place than planned.   (v) 促進. 助長. 推动

Polk→Freeport ↗

84. (A) What is the disadvantage of going to Freeport?   He did his best to further

further 更 (A) It is farther away.   the interest of his state.

(B) It is difficult to return from.

(C) It is too crowded. 太擠了   他竭力增進那個州的利益

營業時間 (D) The store has limited hours.

短   有限的 a man of limited ability 能力不強的人

85. (D) Look at the graphic. Which bus would David like to take?   ✻farther 距離. 時間更遠地、再往前地

(A) The 10:15 to Trallee.   98題 consume

✻limited (B) The 7:00 to Polk City.   ①消耗. 花費 She consumed most of

a limited (C) The 12:00 to Milltown.   her time in reading.

express (D) The 9:30 to Freeport.

                                                            ②吃光. 喝光: The kids soon

9等快車

County Bus Routes			
Avery	8:00	9:15	4:30	5:15
Casper	7:00	7:15	7:30	8:00
Freeport	8:00	9:30	11:00	12:30
Milltown	8:00	10:00	12:00	2:00
Polk City	6:30	7:00	12:00	3:00
Trallee	8:15	9:15	10:15	11:15

limited   consumed all the food
in resources   on the table.

資源有限×   ③燒毀: The fire consumed
                                      half the village.
✻limit   沒有9or10點回程的車
n. 界限、限度. 範圍   且太早出發

Drive slowly within the city limits.   ④使全神貫注. 使著迷. 使憔悴

在市區內車子開慢些   → The boy was consumed with curiosity.
                                      那男孩充滿好奇心

GO ON TO THE NEXT PAGE. ➡

Ladies and gentlemen, the Captain has turned on the Fasten Seat Belt sign. If you haven't already done so, please stow your carry-on luggage underneath the seat in front of you or in an overhead bin. Please take your seat and fasten your seat belt. And also make sure your seat back and folding tray are in their full upright position. If you are seated next to an emergency exit, please read the special instructions card located by your seat carefully. If, in the event of an emergency, you do not wish to perform the functions described, please ask a flight attendant to reseat you. At this time, we request that all mobile phones, pagers, radios and remote controlled toys be turned off for the full duration of the flight, as these items might interfere with the navigational and communication equipment on this aircraft. We request that all other electronic devices be turned off until we fly above 10,000 feet. We will notify you when it is safe to use such devices. We remind you that this is a non-smoking flight. Smoking is prohibited on the entire aircraft, including the lavatories. Tampering with, disabling or destroying the lavatory smoke detectors is prohibited by law. If you have any questions about our flight today, please don't hesitate to ask one of our flight attendants. Thank you.

86. (B) What is prohibited by law?
    (A) Using laptops in the cabin.
    (B) Tampering with smoke detectors.
    (C) Listening to music on the flight.
    (D) Carry-on luggage.

87. (A) Where does this announcement take place?
    (A) On an airplane.
    (B) At a business meeting.
    (C) On television.
    (D) In a bus station.

88. (B) What should listeners do if they have a question?
    (A) Call the airline.
    (B) Ask a flight attendant.
    (C) Go to the lavatory.
    (D) Complain to the manager.

Before we begin the lecture, I'd like to tell you a little bit about myself. I was born in Russia and moved to the United States with my family when I was three. My father was a doctor, and my mother was a teacher. I have two older brothers and a younger sister. I grew up in Boston, but we moved to Chicago when I was 12. I've been interested in science my whole life, so I was ecstatic to receive a scholarship here at Northwestern University to study biology. After earning my bachelor's degree, I got a master's at Stanford. I stayed on there as a researcher for about six years before moving back to Illinois and joining Bio-Tech. I was with Bio-Tech for 10 years before leaving last year to start my own research company, GreenEarth. We employ six full-time researchers, and in the past year we've made a couple of exciting new discoveries, which I'm going to tell you about in just a minute. First, though, I just want to thank the Northwestern president, John Roche, and the faculty of the biology department for inviting me back to speak to you today. It's an exciting moment, and I'm honored.

89. (C) What will the speaker most likely talk about next?
   (A) Sports.
   (B) The weather.
   (C) Biology.
   (D) Economics.

90. (D) Where did the speaker obtain his master's degree?
   (A) Bio-Tech.
   (B) University of Illinois.
   (C) Northwestern University.
   (D) Stanford University.

91. (C) Where was the speaker born?
   (A) Boston.
   (B) Chicago.
   (C) Russia.
   (D) Illinois.

GO ON TO THE NEXT PAGE.

你是否聽過一個故事關於一隻驢子試圖在兩捆乾草中選一捆?

Have you heard the story about the donkey who is trying to choose between two bales

乾草　　　兩捆草在任何方面都是一樣的　　　　尺寸　品質　量　　味道

of hay? Both bales of hay are equal in all respects. Size, quality, amount, fragrance,

你說的出來的都一樣。　兩捆絕對沒有任何差別　　　　　驢子站在這看向左邊

you name it. Absolutely no difference between the two. So the donkey, he's standing

有一捆完美的乾草　　　　　　　然後他看向右邊

there and he looks left. There's a perfectly good bale of hay. Then he looks right.

另一捆美麗的乾草　　　可憐的驢子　　他很困惑不知該左或右

Aha! Another beautiful bale of hay. This poor donkey, he's so confused that he

所以他什麼事都沒做

doesn't know what to do—so he doesn't do anything. He stands there between the

他站在兩捆乾草中間然後餓死了　　　　把大部分的消費者都像那隻

two bales of hay and starves to death. Think of the average consumer as being that

大家都知道的驢子一樣　　　　普遍消費者被這這麼多 而無法做決定

proverbial donkey. The average consumer is so overwhelmed by choice that he can't

而這是你的工作，你的任務，你的熱忱　去創造一捆

make a decision. And it's your job, it's your mission, it's your passion, to create a bale

草，超級 優於其他捆的草　　　　　沒有任何一隻頭腦正常的驢子會不選那捆

of hay so incredibly superior to the others that no donkey in his right mind would pass

若這不是你的熱忱所在。　你就該離這研討會　　✗ pass up 放棄

it up. And if it isn't your passion, then you should walk out of this seminar, demand a

要求退款 在註冊台。　　　然後回去當那個無法下決定的小驢子

refund at the registration desk, and go back to being that indecisive little donkey,

因為我正在浪費你的時間。 ✗ donkey, mule, ass Don't be a young mule.

because I'm wasting your time here. 別那麼固執

---

92. (**D**) Who is the speaker? ✗ speech　語言治療

therapy (A) A preacher. 傳教士　　occupational 職業療法　　專家 therapist

n. 治療 (B) An animal therapist. 動物治療師 physical 物理治療

療法 (C) An author of comic books. 漫畫書作者　 ✗ therapy n. 治療, 療法

(D) An advertising professional. 廣告專家　　 ✗ comparison

advertise v.　　　　　　　　　　　　　ㄋ ㄠ

93. (**A**) Why does the speaker tell the story of the donkey?

insult v.　　　　　　　　　　　　　n. 比較, 對照, 類似

insult n. (A) To draw a comparison. 做比較

→ to make (B) To explain a procedure. 解釋過程 → Here's a bigger size for comparison.

(C) To clarify a statement. 澄清一個立場 ✗ statement n. 陳述, 說明

insults about sb. (D) To insult an audience member. 羞辱觀眾 → The details of the agreement

一般消費者怎樣?　　　　　　　　　　need more exact statement.

94. (**B**) What does the speaker say about average consumers? 協議的細節

✗ prefer (A) They look like donkeys. → 戰勝 覆蓋, 淹沒　需要更確切的說明

較喜歡 (B) They are overwhelmed by choice. 選擇太多　　③ 銀行報告單

寧可(選擇) (C) They prefer smaller bales of hay. 比較喜歡小細的草 I get a bank statement

(D) They have a passion for creativity. 有創意的熱情 every month.

✗ proverbial

adj. 諺語的, 眾所皆知的 → Their generosity is proverbial.

✗ proverb n. 諺語 → Haste makes waste is a proverb. 欲速則不達是句諺語

✗ starve ① 挨餓 ② 渴望 The plants are starving for water. 植物極需水

老實說　　我主要的電腦啟發　　來自於 我對別家電腦公司的服務

Well, to be honest, George, my main inspiration came from being so disappointed with

很失望　　　　　　　　　　　有好多年我採用 Bell PC

customer service from other computer companies. For years I had a Bell PC and

而且每一次有事發生, 解決問題就像是惡夢一場

anytime something went wrong, resolving the issue was a nightmare. Their tech

他們的技術沒支援和客服很可悲.(花稽)　所以我就想

support and customer service was pathetic. And so I thought, well, you know, if you

若你想要做好某事, 你得自己來　　我知道這是老生常談

want something done right, you have to do it yourself. I know it's cliched but I really

但我真的覺得我能比直接的競爭者們做得更好

believed that I could do a better job than the guys who are now my direct competitors.

客戶想要的公司.品牌是他們相信可以履行承諾的　　　履行. 實現

Consumers want companies and brands that they believe will deliver on their promises.

那正是我覺得我可以做出差異的地方　　在客服方面

That's where I felt like I could make a difference: in customer service, because if we

因為若我們能提供更高階的客服　　能激起信任感

can provide a higher level of customer service, that inspires trust in our consumers,

並給我們一個競爭優勢

and gives us a competitive advantage.

鼓舞.喚起 His encouraging words (remarks)
inspired confidence in me.

95. (A) What is the speaker mainly discussing?

industry (A) His reason for starting a business. 開始做生意的理由

工業.企業.行 (B) His political views. 他的政治觀點 → politician 政治家, 政客
勤勉 業 (C) His experience with computers.
(D) His opinion of the computer industry. 他對電腦產業的想法
→ Industry and thrift favor success.
節儉有助於成功 他說消費者如何?
※ competitive adj.

96. (B) What does the speaker say about consumers?
競工
competent (A) They don't care about customer service. 不在乎客戶服務　愛競爭的
有能力的 (B) They prefer reliable companies. 比較喜歡可靠的公司　競爭性的
稱職的 (C) They give him a competitive edge. 給他一個競爭優勢 = competitive advantage
合格的 (D) They always think they can do a better job. 他們總覺得他們能做的更好
說話語說他的公司如何?

97. (A) What does the speaker imply about his company?
(A) They provide a high level of customer service. 提供高品質的客服
※edge (B) They are most concerned with competitive pricing. 最擔心(在乎)
n.邊.緣 (C) They are struggling. 在努力奮鬥中　　　有競爭的定價
尖銳,優勢(D) They are wildly profitable. 獲利很多

→ They lived in a house on the edge of a forest. 住在森林邊的房子裡
→ His remark has a biting edge to it. 他的話非常尖酸辛辣.

v. 徐徐移動.漸進
→ She edged to the front of the crowd.　　※struggle v.努力.奮鬥
→ She edged her chair nearer to the fireplace. → They struggled for peace.
→ She struggled to keep back the tears.

GO ON TO THE NEXT PAGE.

所有美國人都知道　　7月4号並不是真正关於愛國
As all Americans know, the Fourth of July isn't really about being patriotic—it's an excuse
這是在屋頂或者後院烤肉的藉口　喝起多的酒　　　大量的多量的
to have a rooftop or backyard barbeque, to consume copious amounts of
看起棒的煙火　　　　　　　　那住在台北的美國人
alcohol, and to watch some fantastic fireworks. So what are Americans living in Taipei
該做什麼來取代這些行之有年的傳統呢?(由來已久的)　首先　不要期沒
supposed to do in place of these time-honored traditions? For starters, don't expect
有煙火　　但DO要以期待　　和朋友們在DC喝一杯
fireworks. But DO look forward to having drinks with friends at Dazzling Champagne
2/4的派對上　　　只要穿红,白,藍在身上就可得到免費酒
bar's 4th of July party. Free shots will be served to anyone wearing red, white, and
帶上休的朋友　　　若他們不是美國人　　簡單告訴他們
blue. So grab your friends, and if they're not American, brief them on why July 4th is
為何7/4是特殊的日子　並且來DC加入我們開心的玩一晚,並慶祝
a special day and come join us at Dazzling Champagne for a night of fun and
入場免費.並且還有開胃菜
celebration! Admission is free and appetizers will be served. *brief

＊Independence Day. the Fourth of July 美國獨立紀念日　adj.短暫的.簡略的

98. (A) What is the purpose of this announcement? 這個宣佈的目的為何?

    (A) To announce an event. 宣佈活動　　　n.摘要.簡報

    (B) To sell a product. 銷售商品　　　v.作~摘要.簡報

    (C) To start an argument. 開啟討論

    (D) To introduce a speaker. 介紹一個說話者(演講者)　*The commander briefed his man.*

99. (B) What is implied about the 4th of July? 指揮官告訴手下該做哪些事。

major ↔ (A) It's a minor religious holiday. 一個小的宗教的假日

minor   (B) It's an important American holiday. 重要的美國假日

adj.較小的 (C) It's an excuse to set fires. 放火的藉口 → *He was crazy and*

次要的 (D) It's a reason to become an American. 成為美國人的理由 *set the house on fire.*

得到免費的一杯酒者要怎麼做?
100. (C) What should customers do if they want a free shot?

    (A) Bring at least three friends. 帶到3位朋友　*＊in advance*

n.未成年人 (B) Buy an appetizer. 買份開胃菜　　→ *The guard of honor*

副修科目 (C) Wear something red, white, and blue. 穿一些红,白,藍 *marched*

You can't (D) Pay the admission fee in advance. 要付入場費 *in advance.*

serve n.進入許可.入場費.承諾.坦白　預先/在前面　　儀隊走在前面

drinks → *He made an admission that he had used threatening behavior.*

to minors.　他承認用了恐嚇手段

    ＊admissive adj.入場的.入會的.認可的.容許的

    ＊admit v.承認.容許.准許進入　　　　　adj.能幹的

    → We have to admit that he is a highly competent man.

    → The theater admits 1000 people. 容納1000人

    → This matter admits of no delay. 這事不容耽擱.

READING TEST

In the Reading test, you will read a variety of texts and answer several different types of reading comprehension questions. The entire Reading test will last 75 minutes. There are three parts, and directions are given for each part. You are encouraged to answer as many questions as possible within the time allowed.

You must mark your answers on the separate answer sheet. Do not write your answers in your test book.

PART 5

Directions: A word or phrase is missing in each of the sentences below. Four answer choices are given below each sentence. Select the best answer to complete the sentence. Then mark the letter (A), (B), (C), or (D) on your answer sheet.

101. The last bus to Taichung ------- at 11:30.
 (A) departs
 (B) depart
 (C) departing
 (D) to depart

102. Remember kids: don't answer the door for anyone ------- you know who they are.
 (A) except
 (B) unless
 (C) because
 (D) instead

103. The event is ------- the public, with proceeds from ticket sales benefiting a children's art education fund.
 (A) open on
 (B) opened at
 (C) opening of
 (D) open to

104. His stories are so colorful that they defy ------- .
 (A) landing
 (B) applause
 (C) description
 (D) change

105. A newly ------- Spanish-language channel called Latino TV is wholly dedicated to traveling.
 (A) launching
 (B) launce
 (C) launched
 (D) launch

106. The museum has an amazing ------- of Vincent van Gogh's artwork.
 (A) handicap
 (B) collection
 (C) directive
 (D) tasting

107. Marty can play guitar ------- piano.
 (A) because of
 (B) by and by
 (C) if not for
 (D) as well as

108. Taking the flu seriously also ------- taking annual vaccinations seriously.
 (A) involves
 (B) requests
 (C) kneels
 (D) confirms

14

109. When it comes to life insurance, it ------- to quit smoking. 當談到壽險

(A) spits 吐 ← 要付出的代價是戒烟
(B) runs 吐痰語 (戒烟比較好)
(C) pays *it pays to - it produces good results*
(D) longs *long for a chance* 渴望机会 *to do a particular thing*

pays

C

110. Life is a ------- struggle; there is no easy ------- to success. 生活就是持續的奮鬥

(A) constant ; path 沒有成功的捷徑
(B) pleasant ; line 愉悦的
(C) mindless ; button 欠考慮的, 不需动脑的
(D) career ; step 鈕扣≠ bottom 底部

constant *path*

A

111. The noise coming from next door ------- their romantic dinner.

(A) closed 隔壁傳來的噪音打擾了他們
(B) invited 的浪漫晚餐
(C) upgraded v.使分裂, 中断, 瓦解
(D) disrupted *The heavy storm has disrupted telephone service.* 執行 表演

disrupted break

D

112. Mr. Peterson has already learned to send e-mails and chat with friends on social media. Peterson 先生已經學會用社群媒体

(A) yet 寄郵件和聊天
(B) already
(C) no 118(A) contemptuous → contempt n.輕視
(D) ever adj.瞧不起的, 藐视的 →藐视舆论
→ *He is contemptuous of public opinion.*

B

113. Jason smiled and waved as he walked ------- 當他走過呼他微笑並揮手

(A) instead 118(B) contemplate
(B) from a ↓ temple v.默想
(C) found
(D) past *Are you contemplating marriage?* 考慮

past

D

114. Seth doesn't seem to be ------- failing another exam. 她看起來不擔心搞砸另一個考試

(A) combined with → *The two old schools are to combine to form one new school.*
(B) complained to 結合 拘怨
(C) concerned about 擔心
(D) contracted by adj.收缩的: a contracted brow 氣量小的: a contracted mind

about

C

115. The weather forecast ------- more rain and wind. 氣象預報預測会有更多

(A) demands 風雨 要求.命令
(B) respects
(C) calls for =predicts
(D) remembers

calls for

C

116. You must study hard for the college entrance exam. There is a lot ------- 你一定要認真讀入學考試. 有很多要紧

(A) of cake a piece of cake 容易的事
(B) to take → 有風險.有要紧
(C) at stake = in danger ⇔ out of danger
(D) to break

at stake

C

117. After the war, many radicals and traitors were ------- 戰爭之後, 懷著激進分子和叛徒都被処死

(A) completed adj.根本的.激進的
(B) executed follow n.激進分子 ≠ radicle
(C) made v.執行.實施.処死 幼根
(D) performed → execution → executive

executed
B 誠

118. All those daydreams were only -------; they disappeared one by one.

(A) contemptuous 那些白日夢像是暫時
(B) contemplate 的.一個個的消失
(C) temporary adj.臨時的 n.臨時工
(D) contemporary adj.當代的.同齡的

temporary

C

119. One of the ------- aspects of the new headquarters is its closeness to the downtown area. 新總部其中一個令人

(A) pleasing 動(事) 滿意的部分
(B) pleased 被动(人) 是離市區很近
(C) pleases → *I'm very pleased to inform you that your application has been accepted.*
(D) please

A

120. Greg keeps a detailed ------- of all his personal financial transactions.

(A) credit Greg 保留了詳细的
(B) bank 他所有的財務易紀錄
(C) account
(D) receipt 收付店 n.解释.說明.描述

account

C

GO ON TO THE NEXT PAGE.

121. With pleasant weather, breathtaking views and a ------- tourist industry, California's 1,350 miles of sunny shoreline are a significant source of commerce and state pride.
(A) well-furnished
(B) well-developed
(C) well-beloved
(D) well-adjusted

B
有舒服的天氣 漂亮的風景 和發展完善的 旅遊業。加洲有1350哩 長的陽光海岸是重要的 貿易資源和加州之光
裝備齊全的
發展良好的
受人愛的
調程好的

122. Raised in Panama, 41-year-old ------- Hannah Hooper first moved to New York to study fashion merchandise at the Parsons School of Art and Design.
(A) architect n. 建築師
(B) architecture n. 建築
(C) art
(D) arcade 拱廊.長廊商場

A
巴拿馬長大. 41歲的 建築師最初搬到 紐約學習服裝 營銷

123. Although Mr. Darby is a good counselor, a few changes in his approach ------- both him and his clients.
(A) should disturb
(B) might terrify
(C) would benefit
(D) have enrich

C
雖然 Darby 是個好的顧問 (諮詢師) 但他方法做一些改變 對自己和客户都是好的。
=adviser =guidance
打擾
使害怕
受益
使豐富
a counselor to the ambassador
→ Music can enrich your life.

124. You will report ------- to the manager and you will be responsible for supervising the work of engineers and designers.
(A) direct v. I want to dispose of
(B) directly adv. these old books.
(C) direction n. ✗ revoke → The police revoked
(D) directed p.t. his driver's license.

B
你值接向經理回報, 而你負責監督工程師和設計師的工作. 撤回
配置處理
常銷毀照

125. Shouting profanities is not a(n) ------- response to this situation.
(A) live
(B) casual
(C) suggestive 示意的 → His behavior was
(D) appropriate   suggestive of a cultured man.

D
大喊不好聽的語言並不是對這個情况適合 的回應
profanity 不敬的言語
暗示的
adj. 適當的. 恰當的
舉止暗示他是一個有教養的人
→ She picked up a dress appropriate for the occasion.

126. You realize that looking good on the outside isn't necessarily ------- being healthy, don't you?
(A) at length with
(B) the same as
(C) to part with
(D) as told to

B
你明白外在看起來 好看和真正健康 並不必然相等.吧?
最終 At length the bus arrived, 40 minutes late.
→放棄,辭退,與~分別
衰退、後退

127. Unfortunately, those who suffer during an economic recession are typically the poorest members of society.
(A) this
(B) that
(C) them
(D) those

D
adv. 典型地
不穩定地
一貫地
那些遭受經濟蕭條的人,
通常是社會中比較窮的人

128. Though this week's sales were relatively high, the stock price of Linda's Toys continued to fall.
(A) height n. 高度
(B) high adj. adv. n.
(C) highly adv. 高度地.非常
(D) heighten v. 加高.增高

B
雖然這週的銷售相對的高. Linda's 玩具 的股票價格持續下降
→ They are highly skilled workers.
He speaks highly of you.
→ heighten a wall 加高牆

129. Throughout the course of the experiment, we can quickly ------- the relationship between temperature and volume by changing the value for one or the other.
(A) revoke
(B) dispose
(C) establish
(D) found

C
establish
在整個實驗的過程中 我們可以很快的建立 溫度和量的關係.藉由 改變 A or B 的數值。
建立

130. Anderson spoke with actress Mayim Bialik, who holds a Ph.D. in neuroscience.
(A) holded
(B) hold
(C) holding
(D) holds

D
holds
神經科學
他和女演員 M 說話
M 在精神科學領域中 有博士學位。
Ph.D.= Doctor of Philosophy
MBA= Master of Business Administration
BBA= Bachelor of Business Administration.

PART 6

Directions: Read the texts that follow. A word, phrase, or sentence is missing in parts of each text. Four answer choices are given below each of the texts. Select the best answer to complete the text. Then mark the letter (A), (B), (C), or (D) on your answer sheet.

Questions 131-134 refer to the following advertisement.

Is your fur baby looking a little shaggy these days? ------

Perfect Pet has the solution! We offer full grooming services **131.**

for any breed of dog, including Heinz 57. Our groomers have

experience with ------ cuts from classic poodle to English

133.

sheepdog. We also offer bathing, teeth cleaning, and nail

trimming. So bring in your pup today and take home a Perfect

Pet. Services are available ------ or on a walk-in basis.

134.

Perfect Pet

126 Main Street

(across from Bailey Supermarket)

Phone: 589-2000

Hours: 9am-7pm

131. (A) Does your coat have unsightly stains on it
(B) This is the new style this year
(C) Does your dog absolutely hate baths
(D) Of course, babies should not wear fur

132. (A) make
(B) offer
(C) distribute
(D) afford

133. (A) a couple of
(B) the number of
(C) both of
(D) a variety of

134. (A) as soon as possible
(B) by appointment
(C) with nomination
(D) on the fly

GO ON TO THE NEXT PAGE.

17

Questions 135-138 refer to the following e-mail.

To:	All administrative staff
From:	Frank Wheeler
Subject:	New printing facilities
Date:	May 15, 2020

Callum Corporation has installed new printers and copiers in Suites 814, 1002, and 1206. These ------- will be operational as of Monday, May 18. The IT department has installed the printers on the PCs of all administrative assistants. You will be able to print remotely from your workstations. You should use the printing suite on the floor that is closest to your workstation. You will ------- that the printers have been named 8A, 8B, 10A, and so on, to ------- their location. As always, printers and copiers may be used for company business only.

Frank Wheeler
Office Manager

135. (A) abilities
(B) administrators
(C) facilities
(D) institutions

136. (A) find
(B) determine
(C) notify
(D) require

137. (A) notice
(B) discover
(C) involve
(D) reflect

138. (A) If your company has any business, please call the number below.
(B) In that case, you should ask your assistant for a new printer.
(C) If you experience any technical difficulties, please contact the IT department.
(D) All printers will be on sale until the end of the them month.

Questions 139-142 refer to the following announcement.

Dear friends and patrons, *[handwritten: We have special offer for our regular patrons. 老顧客有給特別優惠]*

[handwritten: n.贊助者,主顧]

Your support for the St. Simons Bakery has been outstanding. *[handwritten: 您一直以來對我們的支持都很傑出 (買過很多)]*

[handwritten: Thanks to you 感謝你, 讓我生意越來越好] -------, we have enjoyed a booming business. That means we have *[handwritten: 意味著 我們已成長超過]*
139.

[handwritten: outgrown] ------- our current location. In order to continue to serve you in a *[handwritten: 目前的地點(店太小,生意太好)為了持續服務你們在]*
140.

clean and comfortable environment, we are moving to a new—and *[handwritten: 一個乾淨,舒服的環境裡 我們要搬到一個新的 而且]*

much larger!—location. Our new store is just two blocks away on *[handwritten: 更大的點 我們的新店 在Mill街上隔二個街口遠]*

Mill Street, between First and Second Avenue. In order to ------- the *[handwritten: 在1和2大街中間 facilate]*
141.

move, we will be closed for three days, from August 1 – August 3. *[handwritten: 為了促進搬家,我們會關門3天 8/1~8/3]*

We will have a Grand Opening at our new location on August 4 *[handwritten: 8/4好就會在新底址盛大開幕]*

with free coffee and samples of our delicious baked goods. *[handwritten: 有免費咖啡和我們好吃的烘焙商品試吃 和開幕資訊有關]*
142.

Our store hours will remain the same: 7:00 am – 8:00 pm. *[handwritten: 營業時間保持不變]*

[handwritten notes:]
(B) facilitate v.使促進、容易、幫助   (C) dedicate v.奉獻→ dedication
facilitation n.簡易化.促進.使人方便的物 (CD) collaborate v.合作,句結合
facility n 設備   with power. force → collaboration
*   → to collaborate with sb. in doing sth.*
否定放句首,後面倒裝 S+V. ⟷ V+S.
→ At no-time should you give up studying.

139. (A) At no time 絕不 → We shall know
C (B) In due course 最終   the results of
(C) Thanks to you   the examination
(D) Begging your pardon In due course.
抱歉.請原諒

141. (A) motivate v.給~動机.刺激
B (B) facilitate → motivation
(C) dedicate
(D) collaborate
[handwritten: 到時候就會知道考試的結果 → 期待見到你]

140. (A) outdone outdo 勝過 超越
D (B) outlived 比~活得長 she outlived
(C) outworked   her husband by 20 years.
(D) outgrown outgrow 長大感覺便不再~

142. (A) We look forward to seeing you there
A (B) You can move in at any time 何時都可搬進來
(C) We expect you to come on time
(D) We can all get along with the new
manager 我們都可以和經理們拥進

[handwritten: outgrow one's clothes 個子太了衣服穿不了]
[handwritten: Don't worry, he'll outgrow it. 別擔心.等他長大就會好的]
[handwritten: 融洽 (C) 我們希望你可以準時到)]

GO ON TO THE NEXT PAGE.

*possess

Adam Williamson
1246 Maple Drive
Springfield, MA 50119

擁有·持有·具有·佔有
有豐富礦藏
→ The country possesses rich mineral deposits.
→ One main idea possessed her, 她只有一個想法 she must get away from home.

Dear Mr. Williamson,

在檢查了我們的紀錄後 我們注意到你有3本書 in possession of
After examining our records, we noticed that you are ------- three books
143.
已經大超過歸還時間了 如您所知, majority
that are considerably overdue for return. As you know, the ------- of our
144.
我們大部分的書可以借出兩週 你也可以把書留久一點
books may be checked out for two weeks. You may keep the books longer if
若你想要, 但你必需來圖書館延長借用時間
you wish, but you must come into the library to extend the lending time. In
除此之外, 沒有在到期日內歸還的書本 incur
addition, books that are not returned by their due date ------- fines of 25 cents
145.
每天每本書會有25分的罰款, 你的書目前超過三週 趕快來處理
per day per book. Your books are currently three weeks overdue. ------- If
146.
若有任何問題, 歡迎電話聯絡
you have any questions, feel free to contact me by phone.

Sincerely,

145 (A) infer v.推斷·猜想·意味著
→ I infer that my favorite proposal has been accepted.

Rosemary Evans
Head Librarian
Springfield Lending Library

(B) imply v.暗示·暗指·必然包含
Her silence implied consent. 他的沉默意味著同意
Rights imply duties. 權利必包含義務

(D) incur v.招致 She incurred his wrath.
她落得他發火

143. (A) having
C (B) in need of 急需 He is in need of money.
(C) in possession of 擁有 Who is in possession
(D) overtime with of this?

→ 多數：The majority were on Tom's side.

144. (A) most
B (B) majority
(C) percentage He won by a majority
(D) number 以兩票多出獲勝 of two.

律.成人：A person reaches his majority at the age of 21. 21歲達到法定年齡.

145. (A) infer
D (B) imply
(C) invest 投資·耗費(時間·金錢)
(D) incur 解決這個問題

146. (A) I will visit the client in the afternoon 我下去看去拜訪客戶 (D) 請盡快到圖書館
D (B) Please bring your bag to the office
(C) I forgot to mention that you look good today 我忘記說你今天看起來很不錯
(D) Please visit the library at your earliest convenience to resolve this issue

Directions: In this part you will read a selection of texts, such as magazine and newspaper articles, e-mails, and instant messages. Each text or set of texts is followed by several questions. Select the best answer for each question and mark the letter (A), (B), (C), or (D) on your answer sheet.

Questions 147-148 refer to the following advertisement.

A Christmas Concert
At the National Concert Hall

Address: No. 21 Zhōngshān S. Road,
Zhōngzhèng District, Taipei

Time: December 24 at 7:30 pm

Price at door: 800 TWD

Prepaid Price: 500 TWD

Phone: (02) 2578-6731

Renowned Canadian conductor Howard Dyck leads the Taipei Symphony Orchestra in a family-friendly Christmas concert that will fill your heart with Christmas cheer! Don't miss this holiday treat!

147. What is the purpose of this ad?
(A) To sell a product.
(B) To promote a concert.
(C) To announce a new holiday.
(D) To recruit potential employees.

148. Where will the event be held?
(A) The National Concert Hall.
(B) 7:30 p.m.
(C) 800 TWD.
(D) December 24.

GO ON TO THE NEXT PAGE.

Summer is the best time to return to school!
你需要更好的生意技巧而我們能幫助你
You need better business skills and we can help.

每個夏天. Rockland 大學企管系提供

Each summer Rockland College of Business Administration offers
將此課程給 有經驗的 管理者 提案精進

special courses for experienced managers who want to sharpen their
他們目前生意技巧 或是學習新方法的 你將會和同儕

existing business skills or learn new ones. You will study with your
各在一個一周的強加課程(密集) 模擬了

peers in a week-long intensive session that simulates the world of
國際貿易的世界 將會學習新理論 和所議周边世界的

international commerce. You will learn new theories and study
市場趨勢 之前上过课的學生

market trends from around the world. Students in previous sessions
發現這個知識馬上可運用在他們目前的工作情况中

have found this knowledge to be immediately applicable to their

current work situations. adj. 合用的.可應用的、合適的. 可實施的

每間公司只有一位學生能 被這門特殊課程接受 apply v. 運用.實施.敷

Only one student per company is accepted into this special program.

All applications require three letters of recommendation and

employment <u>verification</u>. 所有的申請者需要三封推薦函和在職証明

*sharpen /verify v.3證明.核對.核实 His prediction was verified.

/ˈʃɑrpn/ For more information, call the **Summer Training Center** 他的預訂得到

v.削尖.磨快,使尖銳 College of Business Administration 証实

Cold weather sharpens the pain Rockland College → It was easy to verify

in my knee. 寒冷使我膝盖 his statements.

* recommend (212)372-3477 規則 他的强張容易

疼痛加劇 遵守 征实

→ I recommend you to comply with safety regulations.

→ His proposal has much to recommend it. 他的建議有不少可取之處

→ I recommend my child to her care. 我把孩子托付給她照顧

149. Who would most likely be interested in
B this advertisement?
  (A) Office clerks. 辦公室員工
  (B) Professional managers. 專業經理人
  (C) College professors. 大學教授
  (D) Undergraduate students. 未畢業的學生

150. What is required for admission? 〈成績〉
C (A) Your college transcripts. 大學證明書
  (B) Your college diploma. 大學文憑
  (C) Three letters of recommendation. 3封推薦信
  (D) Above average test scores. 高於平均考試成績

* transcript n.抄本.副本
A→B write

*recommend v.介紹、建議.勸告.付託(UP)

menu

Lounge Bar

garlic bread 大蒜麵包		2.50
fat chips =thick-cut French fries		5.00
potato wedges 薯角		6.00
rib fillet steak sandwich w chips 豬肋排三明治		11.00
cajun chicken strips w salad & chips 肯瓊雞		11.00
bangers & mash w vegetables 香腸		11.00
garlic prawns w rice 蒜蝦		12.00
rissoles w sweet potato mash & vegetables 炸肉餅		11.00
roasted pumpkin, spinach & ricotta 軟酪		
ravioli w parmesan cream sauce 義大利餃		12.00
caesar salad 凱撒沙拉 帕瑪森起司		10.00
chicken caesar salad		12.50
roast of the day* 今日烤物	lunch	3.50
*lounge n.休閒室、候机室	dinner	10.00
v.倚靠、閒逛: I saw some people just		
THURSDAY NIGHT SPECIAL lounging about there.		
t-bone, salad & chips*		7.99

prices subject to change

*only available with drink purchase

*strip
n.條、帶、細長片：There is a strip of garden behind his house. 房子後面有塊狹長形園地
v.剝、奪、脫→The boy stripped to the waist. 男孩打赤膊
It was wrong of him to strip his daughter of the right to education. 不該剝奪女兒受教育的權利

151. What is the least expensive item on the menu? 最便宜的品項

adj. He has least money of all of us.
adv. He works least. 他工作得最少
This is the least useful of the four books. 這一本最無用
n. 最少、最小 Giving him food was the least we could do.

(A) Garlic bread. 大蒜麵包
(B) Fat chips.
(C) Roast of the day at lunch.
(D) Potato wedges. 馬鈴薯角 楔子

wedge issue 爭端問題、製造分裂的問題

152. What is the most expensive item on the menu? 最貴的

(A) Garlic prawns with rice.
(B) Chicken Caesar Salad.
(C) Roast of the day at dinner.
(D) Ravioli with parmesan cream sauce.

GO ON TO THE NEXT PAGE.

*resistance n. 抵抗 I catch cold frequently because my resistance
back / stand
again / 抵抗力 is low.
against

Dear Libby,   → resistant adj. 抵抗的.抗~的   water resistant 防水的
                                              heat resistant 耐熱的
我24歲大學畢業有學士學歷—刑事司法系   rust resistant 防銹的

I am 24 and graduated from college with a bachelor's degree in

我目前和父母同住   n. 單數.學士
criminal justice. I am currently living with my parents. They are a

他們有點愛控制而且討厭我的拒絕   我成長過程中做所有他們
bit controlling and hate resistance from me. I grew up doing

要我做的事,沒有個人的意見
everything they told me with no personal opinions of my own, until

直到一年前我認識了未婚夫   他幫助我得到勇氣去表達和讓我的想法
I met my fiance a year ago. He has helped me gain the strength to

被知道(被聽見) n. 力.力量.實力.效力
speak up and let my thoughts be known.   →The medicine has lost its strength.

我們正試著存錢住在一起   → He hasn't got enough strength to remove
                                                              that
We're trying to save enough money to live together. Mom has   stone.

媽表達很清楚她不喜歡這个想法   因為我們尚未結婚
made it clear that she doesn't like that idea because we're not

她跟爸很不開心我不再我的學位領域內工作
married yet. She and Dad are also unhappy that I no longer want to

我在警長勤務室工作過幾個月
work in the field my degree is in. (I worked for a sheriff's office for

但是被糟糕的對待   接著我被革取了
a couple of months and was treated horribly, and then I was fired.)

我一直告訴爸媽這是我的生活   adv.可怕地   但看起來
I have told my parents repeatedly that this is my life, but it

似乎沒有幫助   你有任何建議關於我該跟他們說什麼
seems to do no good. Do you have any suggestions on what I

關於這些問題?   n.問題.爭議.發行物.期刊
should say to them about these issues?

                                                    v.發行.核發.流出 Lava issued
                                                                    from the volcano.
– GROWN-UP GIRL IN GEORGIA ↙

*issue n.問題.爭議.發行(物);(報刊)期號,這期裡
→ There is an article about Tom in this issue. 有一篇关於Tom的文章
→ He died without issue. 他身後無子女

153. What is Grown-up Girl's main
problem?
(A) Control issues with her daughter.
(B) Control issues with her employer. 老闆
(C) Control issues with her parents. employée
(D) Control issues with her boyfriend. 員工

154. What does Grown-up Girl want to do?
(A) Get married. 結婚
(B) Choose a new major. 選新的主修
(C) Move in with her boyfriend.
(D) Have a child. 搬去和男友同住

* employ 雇用 The factory employs a thousand workers.
使用.利用 How do you employ your spare time? 如何利用空餘時間?

We hate to break it to you, but big companies aren't just going to let a chilly employee crank the heat up whenever he or she pleases. But if they simply locked the thermostat or put the controls out of reach, the employees would constantly complain. The solution: A thermostat that doesn't actually do anything but placate the chilly masses.

In many offices the controls on the wall don't do anything. Some bosses and landlords feel like they can't trust people not to fiddle with the temperature all day and thus cost them money, so they install dummy thermostats which give people the illusion of control. They work really well, as most people fool themselves into believing they feel the change.

When pressed, most technicians tasked with installing the devices admit that they're merely window dressing. A 2010 report by *The Wall Street Journal* quoted one HVAC technician who estimated that 90% of office thermostats were completely fake (though other technicians gave lower estimates). We haven't seen any study confirming that people feel warmer after fiddling with these props. But let's be honest: If they didn't work, offices wouldn't bother installing them.

*fiddle v. 亂動, 胡來 ＊Crank v. 增大
*placate v. 平息, 安撫

155. What is the purpose of the article?
- (A) To expose a little known fact.
- (B) To draw support for a cause.
- (C) To explain a complex procedure.
- (D) To demand an apology.

156. What supports his claim?
- (A) An employee survey.
- (B) Scientific research.
- (C) Public opinion.
- (D) An article in *The Wall Street Journal.*

157. What does the author claim?
- (A) All bosses and landlords are cheap.
- (B) All employees are not to be trusted.
- (C) Most office thermostats are merely props.
- (D) Most HVAC technicians are dishonest.

GO ON TO THE NEXT PAGE.

As the name implies, fast-food is supposed to be, well, *fast*. But have you ever wondered what the fastest fast-food restaurant is? According to Quick Service Restaurant (QSR) Magazine's annual Drive-Thru Performance Study of six national fast-food chains, Wendy's takes the crown with an average 129.75 seconds per transaction. Burger King came in sixth, barely hanging onto its crown with 201.33 seconds. By averaging the times during 318 visits to Wendy's, QSR Magazine found that Wendy's was 20 seconds faster than second-place Taco Bell. The magazine and Insula Research conducted the survey by visiting each restaurant between 203 to 362 times. However, speed may not be everything. The fast-food industry doesn't exactly have an equivalent to the computer chip industry's Moore's law, which predicted in the 1970s that processing power would double every two years. Complex menus have contributed to a plateau in drive-thru speed for the last seven or eight years, the magazine states. A statement from Burger King noted that it "prides itself on providing excellent products and great service to all of our guests."

QSR's other ratings included order accuracy, favorable exterior, condition of landscaping, speaker clarity and customer service. Here is its ranking of restaurants by average service times:

1. Wendy's – 129.75 seconds
2. Taco Bell – 149.69 seconds
3. Bojangles' – 171.61 seconds
4. Krystal – 175.94 seconds
5. McDonald's – 190.06 seconds
6. Burger King – 201.33 seconds

158. What was the main focus of the QSR study?

(A) Average service times.
(B) Affordability.
(C) Order accuracy.
(D) Exterior conditions.

159. What did Moore's Law predict?

(A) Declining customer service.
(B) The growth of computer processing power.
(C) Exploding profit margins.
(D) Improved speaker clarity.

160. What has caused drive-thru service times to plateau?

(A) Complex menus.
(B) Customer complaints.
(C) Longer lines in the drive-thru.
(D) Poorly trained employees.

Memorandum

TO: Kelly Anderson, Marketing Executive
FROM: Jonathon Fitzgerald, Market Research Assistant
DATE: June 14
SUBJECT: Fall Clothes Line Promotion

Market research and analysis show that the proposed advertising media for the new fall line need to be reprioritized and changed. Findings from focus groups and surveys have made it apparent that we need to update our advertising efforts to align them with the styles and trends of young adults today. No longer are young adults interested in television shows. Also, it is has become increasingly important to use the Internet as a tool to communicate with our target audience to show our dominance in the clothing industry.

XYZ Company needs to focus advertising on Internet sites that appeal to young people. According to surveys, 72% of our target market uses the Internet for five hours or more per week. The following list shows in order of popularity the most frequented sites:

- Google
- Facebook
- Myspace
- eBay
- iTunes

Shifting our efforts from our other media sources such as radio and magazine to these popular Internet sites will more effectively promote our product sales. Young adults are spending more and more time on the Internet downloading music, communicating and researching for homework and less and less time reading paper magazines and listening to the radio. As the trend for cultural icons goes digital, so must our marketing plans.

161. What is the main purpose of this memo?
(A) To propose a change to a plan.
(B) To attract young readers.
(C) To announce a new product.
(D) To discipline a group of employees.

162. Who wrote the memo?
(A) A marketing executive.
(B) An advertising sales person.
(C) A market research assistant.
(D) A group of concerned adults.

163. According to the memo, which of the following is the most popular website?
(A) Google.
(B) Facebook.
(C) eBay.
(D) iTunes.

GO ON TO THE NEXT PAGE.

Questions 164-167 refer to the following article.

WHO Health Guidelines for Your Pre-Schooler

Nothing is more important than your child's health. [1] This week, the World Health Organization released new guidelines for the youngest of our children, those under the age of five. In general, the guidelines say that children should both move more and sleep more. [2] Specifically, kids between the ages of one and four should be physically active for at least three hours a day. Infants should also be active several times a day. As every parent knows, getting enough sleep is key to growing up healthy both physically and mentally. Four-year-olds generally need 10 to 12 hours of sleep a day, those under the age of one need 12 to 15 hours. What's not included in the WHO guidelines? [3] Screen time. In fact, according to the WHO, children aged two to four should spend no more than one hour a day looking at an electronic screen. Kids younger than that shouldn't be watching screens at all. How does one balance that with the demands of young kids for video entertainment? [4] Well, that's what parenting is all about.

164. What is the article about?

(A) How to limit screen time for pre-schoolers.

(B) Tips for raising healthy children.

(C) WHO guidelines on sleep deprivation.

(D) When children should begin using computers.

165. What does the author suggest?

(A) Parents are responsible for following these guidelines.

(B) The WHO guidelines are unrealistic.

(C) It is impossible to make children follow the guidelines.

(D) The WHO should include more practical advice in its guidelines.

166. What does the WHO recommend for a typical two-year-old?

(A) Frequent exercise, but no access to electronic screens

(B) More than an hour a day of television but more than 12 hours of sleep.

(C) No television at all and more exercise and sleep.

(D) Three hours of physical activity and at least 10 hours of sleep each day.

167. In which of the positions marked [1], [2], [3], and [4] does the following sentence best belong?

"It is worthwhile, therefore, to listen to the experts."

(A) [1]

(B) [2]

(C) [3]

(D) [4]

28

Silver was the most popular exterior car color in America for nearly a decade. But while it remains beloved by automotive designers for best showing off a car's styling, it was finally overthrown this year by white. According to Sandy McGill, BMW Designworks' lead designer in color, materials, and finish, this is Steve Jobs' doing. "Prior to Apple, white was associated with things like refrigerators or the tiles in your bathroom. Apple made white valuable."

Valuable, yet boring. Fortunately, our expert interviews and analysis reveal that more enticing colors are emerging.

Light blue's ascension is connected to environmental wellbeing: clear skies, clean water. Crisp oranges are migrating from the world of high-end outdoor equipment. New paint technology may finally allow fashion's passion for fluorescents to flow from the runways onto the highways. And, as always, the smart money's on gold: as its price and profile have skyrocketed, so has its demand as a coating.

168. Where would this article most likely be found?

(A) A website about cars.
(B) A fashion magazine.
(C) An academic journal.
(D) A marketing report.

169. According to the article, who is responsible for the popularity of the color white?

(A) Automotive designers.
(B) Luxury car dealers.
(C) Insurance companies.
(D) Steve Jobs.

170. What does the author think about the color white?

(A) It is exciting.
(B) It is boring.
(C) It is dangerous.
(D) It is unpopular.

171. Which of the following is not mentioned in the article as an enticing color?

(A) Scarlet red.
(B) Fluorescent.
(C) Light blue.
(D) Gold.

GO ON TO THE NEXT PAGE.

On Monday, July 27th, the residents of the Big Apple witnessed something quite out of this world: three men gracefully flying around the skies of Lower Manhattan. As it turns out, they were not ballet dancers with super human powers, but cleverly camouflaged radio controlled airplanes.

The gimmick was the genius idea of Thinkmodo, a New York-based marketing company that specializes in concocting viral sensations to promote events. This recent one was created to publicize the release of *Chronicle*, a movie about three high-school students who discover they have super powers that include the ability to fly.

The three people-planes each completed six, five-minute flights across the Hudson River. Though "kite-like" in appearance and weight (just 4 lbs. each), the planes were actually sophisticated flying instruments that required some expert maneuvering to ensure a smooth flight. The company therefore summoned the experts from the Academy of Model Aeronautics, who put each radio-controlled aircraft through some rigorous testing prior to the big event.

As you can imagine, the stunt was a huge success, despite the fact that one of the "flying" men seemed to lose his super power mid-flight and had to be fished out of New York City's Harbor Point. Fortunately, for those of us who missed it, there is a great video that captures the salient moments.

This is not the first time Thinkmodo has come up with such a stunt. To promote the recent thriller *Limitless*, they released a video depicting a man using an invention to hack the large video screens that line New York City's Times Square.

172. What is Thinkmodo? 無線電碟控飛機
C (A) A radio-controlled aircraft.
(B) An aerónautics academy. 航空學院
(C) A marketing company. 行銷公司
(D) A movie producer. 電影製作人

173. What did people in Lower Manhattan 的電影
D witness on July 27?
(A) Three ballet dancers in a street brawl. 3位芭蕾舞者在街上爭吵
(B) Three men flying though the sky. 在天空飛
(C) Three men flying a plane. 3人在開飛機
(D) A marketing stunt involving radio-controlled airplanes.

行銷表演包含無線電控制飛機

174. What was Thinkmodo trying to promote? 環境的意識
C (A) Environmental awareness.
(B) Its brand name. 品牌名稱
叫做那能 (C) A movie entitled *Chronicle*.
失控 (D) The Academy of Model Aeronautics. AMA模範航空學院
(非營利組織)

175. What is true about Thinkmodo?
B (A) They had to be fished out of Harbor Point. 要從HP被釣出來
(B) They have done this type of thing before. 以前做過這種表演
(C) They are very picky when choosing clients. 選客戶很排剔
(D) They are a nonprofit corporation. n.大公司
是非營利組織   法人
社團法人
*picky adj. 挑剔的   股份有限公司
She is a picky eater.
她是個挑食的人
She is picky about what she eats because she is on a diet.
他正在節食,所以排食挑得厲害

*stunt
v.阻礙: Lack of pooor food often stunts a child.
缺少食物阻擋小孩生長
n. 矮小的人.樹.絕技.驅險動作.表演
He performs riding stunts in the circus.

193(A) brawl 爭吵.打架.水流峰聲
We could hear the loud brawl of a brook behind the house.
(v.) 爭吵.打架: Usually you could see them, playing or brawling on the street.

*summon 召喚.傳喚.請求.要求
He was summoned to appear in court as a witness.
They had to summon a second conference and change the previous decision.
He summoned up his courage and proposed to her.
鼓起勇氣向她求婚。

*sophisticated adj. 精通的.也故的.有經驗的
*instrument n.儀器.累器.手段. Language is an instrument for communication.
*maneuvering n.謀略.手究. political maneuverings 政治
/məˈnuvəriŋ/   diplomatic   外交 手段

GO ON TO THE NEXT PAGE.

*emigrate v. 移居外國(區) ↔ imigrate v. 遷移.遷入
/'emɪgret/ emigrant   /'ɪmɪgret/   emigration n. 移居(外)
Article 1   移出者 ↔ immigrant   immigration n. 移居(入)
                              移入者

沒有保險的美國居民數字成長到超過4千5百萬
The number of uninsured U.S. residents has grown to over 45

雖然這個數字包含非法移民
million (although this number includes illegal immigrants). Since

自從健保   持續飆費   是通貨膨脹的好几倍
health care premiums continue to grow at several times the rate

很多公司就選擇了不提供健保的方案
of inflation, many businesses are simply choosing not to offer a

或者就算有提供   把更多的成本轉嫁到員工身上
health plan, or if they do, to pass on more of the cost to

員工面對到更高的成本他們自己常選擇不要健保
employees. Employees facing higher costs themselves are often

                                  健康照護變得
choosing to go without health coverage. Health care has become

    超級無法付擔   對公司或是個人而言都是
increasingly unaffordable for businesses and individuals.

    選擇要保留健康保險的公司或個人
Businesses and individuals that choose to keep their health plans

    需要付更高的金額   記住   公司只有
must pay a much higher amount. Remember, businesses only

    一定救量的金額可以花在勞力上(員工)
have a certain amount of money they can spend on labor. If they

    如果公司必須花更多在健保費   #
must spend more on health insurance premiums, they will have

    那就会有更少的身花在加薪.雇用新人   投資 和之類的
less money to spend on raises, new hires, investment, and so on.

    個人需要花更多來支付保費的   有動的錢
Individuals who must pay more for premiums have less money to

    花在租金   食物   和消費商品上   項言之
spend on rent, food, and consumer goods; in other words, less

    更少的錢回歸到經濟體系中   因此.健保
money is pumped back into the economy. Thus, health care

    阻止了國家有強健的經濟復甦(國家無法復甦)
prevents the country from making a robust economic recovery. A

    一個簡單美的 政府控制系統   能減少成本的
simpler government-controlled system that reduces costs would

    可以長遠而言諦助復甦
go a long way in helping that recovery.

*health care 醫療保健

台灣全民健保 National Health Insurance NHI
健康保費 health insurance premium
*premium n. 獎品.獎金

Fannie Mae 美國聯邦國民抵押協會

Article 2

沒有任何一個政府單位或部門能有效運作

There isn't a single government agency or division that runs efficiently; 我們真的希望政府處理像健保這樣複雜的事嗎? do we really want the government handling something as (感嘆詞) 試圖想出一個運作有效率的政府機關 complex as health care? Quick, try to think of one government office (叫) 美國聯邦金融資款抵押公司 that runs efficiently. Fannie Mae and Freddie Mac? The Department 交通部 社会保障 of Transportation? The Social Security Administration? The 教育部 沒有任何一個政府辦公室 Department of Education? There isn't a single government office that 能夠從每一分錢裡擠出效率像私人部門一樣 squeezes efficiency out of every dollar the way the private sector can. 我們都聽過政府花費昂貴之做 We've all heard stories of government waste such as million-dollar 亂牛胳氣的研究 或是五角大廈(國防部)花 14×10億=140億 cow flatulence studies or the Pentagon's 14 billion dollar Bradley 設計做打杖坦克(Bradley Fighting Vehicle) 結果導致一台運輸車 design project that resulted in a transport vehicle which when struck 被迫擊炮打到的時候, 釋放出瓦斯, 結果殺死了裡頭所有人 by a mortar produced a gas that killed every man inside. How about 那美國收入稅系統呢? 當一開始執行時 the U.S. income tax system? When originally implemented, it 從最高收入公民1%中提稅 看今天 collected 1 percent from the highest-income citizens. Look at it today. n年前政府出版了一本"稅務簡化設計" A few years back the government published a "Tax Simplification 而這本書本身超過1000頁 這就是�搞客 Guide," and the guide itself was over 1,000 pages long! This is what 亂搞 一些本該簡單的事所會發生的. happens when politicians mess with something that should be simple. 想想机動車輛管理局 這是很沒有懂的事 Think about the Department of Motor Vehicles. This isn't rocket 他們需要追踪炤照 和基本邦据資料 science—they have to keep track of licenses and basic database 居了美國民. 可是 支持這部門的成本 information for state residents. However, the costs to support the 非常大量 而上次你去車輛管理局都不用排隊是何 department are enormous, and when was the last time you went to 時? the DMV and didn't have to stand in line? If it can't handle things this 這麼簡單的事 如何能期望政府處理所有複雜的. simple, how can we expect the government to handle all the complex 有差別多化的醫療系統事務 若任何私人公司一年又一年的失敗 nuances of the medical system? If any private business failed year 沒有達到設定之目標 並且滿足顧客 after year to achieve its objectives and satisfy its customers, it would 他就會歇業可做 或是被競爭者超越. go out of business or be passed up by competitors.

*nuance
/nju'ɑːns/
n.色調. 聲調. 意義. 見解等
↳ 細微差別

You failed to notice the nuances in his remarks this time. 你不了解他這次話中的細微差別

ON TO THE NEXT PAGE.

176. What is the main difference between the two articles?

C
- (A) Subject matter. 主題不同
- (B) Use of language. 語訊不同
- (C) Opinion. 意見
- (D) There is no difference.

不該相信
政府能控制
醫療照護系統

177. What do both articles agree on? 政府高度有
效率

D
- (A) The government is highly efficient.
- (B) Health care is expensive.
- (C) Taxes are too high. 稅太高
- (D) They don't agree on anything. 不同意任何

178. What does the first article say?

A
- (A) The government should control the health care system. 應要控制
- (B) Taxes should be raised. 稅要提高
- (C) More research is needed. 需要更多研究
- (D) Most people don't have insurance.

大部分人沒保險

179. What does the second article say?

B
- (A) People choose to go without insurance. 人們選擇不保險
- (B) The government should not be trusted to control the health care system. 私以單位會破壞
- (C) The private sector will destroy health care. 健保
- (D) Health insurance is not practical for small businesses. ✗

健保不是只適合小型公司

180. Which of the following is NOT discussed in either article?

D
- (A) Health care.
- (B) Insurance.
- (C) Business.
- (D) Politics.

✗ practical adj. 實踐的
→ Practical experience is often very important.

✗ 186-190 補充   municipal 市的. 市立的. 市政的
Consequence   → He is in charge of the municipal housing project.
①. 結果. 後果 I'm quite willing to accept the consequences.
② 重大. 重要性 He is a man of great conquence.
③ 自大 The young man rambled on with an air of great consequence.
    這年輕人帶著自大的神態浪竟後了的東拉西扯.

Litter
n. ①. 廢棄物 ③ 一窩 (仔畜) A female rat may have five or six litters yearly.
② 雜亂: Her room was in such a litter that she was ashamed to
                                           ask me in.
v. 把~弄得亂t+入精   紙屑
Don't litter up the floor with scraps of paper.
使充滿 (髒亂)
The fire-place was littered with cigarette butts. 壁爐裡都是煙頭
Applaud
v. 鼓掌. 稱讚 We applauded him for his courage. 稱讚他的勇氣

34

Date: Mon, 15 June 2020
To: "Craig Stevenson" <blaze@facebook.com>,
    "David Ward" <geezer@msn.com>,
    "Bob Dobbins" <bobber@aol.com>
From: "Brent Heinrich" <bheinrich@gmail.com>
Subject: Re: Weekend in Hualien

Craig, et al.

I once went on a hiking excursion with heavy weather brewing offshore, and we chose to proceed despite the possibility of heavy rain. We ended up having to call in a rescue team.

The east coast highway is prone to flooding and rockslides, and this is not a joke. So I'd appreciate it if you'd can the mockery, Craig. If the typhoon has passed by this weekend and the coast is clear (literally and figuratively), then fine, let's have a beach party. Otherwise, let's not be chuckleheaded dimwits.

The forecast was for the typhoon to land today, but it has not reached Taiwan yet. That means it's moving slower than expected. The likelihood of a serious storm being on top of the island this weekend is high. If so, I'm not driving down the east coast.

If you choose to do so, I pity those who travel with you. We all know your old clunker has no air-con, and you have to drive with the windows open.

GO ON TO THE NEXT PAGE.

35

Handwritten annotations:

* excursion n. 郊遊. 遠足   * brew 釀造. 計畫. 泡茶. 煮咖啡
out / run
→ A war seems to be brewing between the two countries.
兩國間似乎正醞釀戰爭.

* literally
逐字地、正確地、實在地. 不誇張地
The city was literally destroyed.
那城市真の被毀滅了

* figuratively 比喻的
(就是不管哪方面而言都是完全暗朗的)

Craig, et al. 以及其他人
即將發生   * mockery 嘲笑. 笑柄 假冒 徒勞無功
我曾經有一次去戶外旅行有大的離岸風
我們還是捧前進不管大雨的可能性
我們最後需要叫救援隊來   * can ① 取消

東岸公路可能會淹水和土石流, 這不是開玩笑
若你能取笑這個可笑的行為我會很感激
若颱風這週末通過然後海岸晴朗
那好吧, 我們开派对办派队
不然, 就不要当低能白痴 = stupid people
→ 預報說颱風今天登陸, 但尚未到台灣
意思是比預期得移動不更慢
可能性
這週末強大暴風雨在半島上方的可能性極高
若是如此, 我不开车去東岸 → 若你還是要去. 我可憐那些和你同往
我們都知道你の破車沒有冷氣
你开车时車窗要打开
→ 我們應充分利用一切有利因素

* call in
① 请假 call in sick. ③ 發揮. 調动 We should now call all positive factors into full play.
② 表示怀疑 His honesty was called in question. 是否誠实令人怀疑

Date: Mon, 15 June 2020

To: **Brent Heinrich** <bheinrich@gmail.com>,

"**Craig Stevenson**" <blaze@facebook.com>,

"**Bob Dobbins**" <bobber@aol.com>

From: "**David Ward**" <geezer@msn.com>

Subject: Re: Weekend in Hualien

Brent,

First of all, it's Monday. A lot can happen between now and Friday. Given the general reliability of weather forecasting, there's no reason to panic and cancel the trip unless it is clearly a dangerous storm. If you really want to take the discussion in that direction, I find it funny that you've chosen to ignore the reports which indicate the typhoon isn't coming anywhere near the east coast. (Click here for that report. You're welcome.)

Second, nobody said anything about hiking in remote mountain areas. We're not camping in Taroko Gorge, for God's sake. Remember? We've booked rooms at a beach resort. Golf, swimming, poker, eating and drinking are on the agenda. Finally, even if you had not been sarcastic and bitter toward Craig, your "chuckleheaded dimwits" comment would be offensive if I took anything you say seriously. Your choice of words pretty much sums up your character. Therefore, I personally feel that this trip would be infinitely more enjoyable if you weren't a part of it. So please, honor your promise to stay home.

remote

adj. 冷淡的: she was a silent girl, cool and remote.

remote control 搖控器

reliability n. 可靠.可信賴性(程度)

reliable adj. 可靠的.確實的 → I found this to be a reliable brand of washing machines.

reliably adv. 可靠地

確實地: I was reliably informed that there are no snakes on this island.

首先.今天是週一

今天到週五之間誰知道事都可能發生

有鑑於通常天氣預報可信度都蠻高的

沒有什麼理由需要

驚慌和取消旅行

除非很明顯的是場危險的暴風雨

如果你真的要以那方向來討論

我覺得很好笑.

你還選擇忽略有些颱風不會靠近東岸的報導

連結在這.不用客氣(很嗆)

遙遠的.偏僻的.久遠的 (up)

(That happened in the remote past.)

第二.沒人說要去超遠的山區健行

我們又不是露營在太魯閣露營

拜託

記得嗎

我們在海灘度假村訂房.高爾夫.游泳.

打牌.吃吃喝喝都在行程表上.(不危險)

最後.我算你沒有對Craig態度

"諷刺"又苦言.但你所像公眾蛋呆瓜說自己人的.若我諸真看待你說的

任何話的話

你選擇的用字基本上已經結了你自人的個性

因此

我個人認為這趟旅行

絕對會更有趣若你沒有參與的話.所以拜託

極其.無限地.無窮地 請你兌現你的承諾.好好待在家

That was infinitely better than his last film.

honor v.

①.兌現.貫踐 ②尊敬: He honors his teacher. ③使增光 You honor us with your presence.

offensive adj.令人不喜的.討厭的.覺得冒犯的

你的蒞臨是我們的光榮

181. Who wrote the first e-mail?
(A) Brent Heinrich.
(B) Craig Stevenson.
(C) David Ward.
(D) Bob Dobbins.

延著東岸的公路關閉了
天氣預報幾乎總是正確

182. Who wrote the second e-mail?
(A) Brent Heinrich.
(B) Craig Stevenson.
(C) David Ward.
(D) Bob Dobbins.

adj. 準確的. 精確的

The new salesgirl is accurate at figures. 計算正確無誤

Is your watch accurate? 你的錶準嗎?

183. What does the author of the first e-mail say?
他是糟糕的篤駛
(A) Craig is a terrible driver.
(B) The typhoon will probably miss the east coast. 颱風可能不會到東岸
(C) It is too dangerous to take the trip. 去旅行了太危險了
(D) They need to call in a rescue team.
需要叫救難隊來

184. What does the author of the second e-mail say?
(A) The highways along the east coast are closed.
(B) Weather forecasts are almost always accurate.
(C) Craig isn't going to drive.
(D) Brent should stay home.

185. What is the purpose of the trip?
(A) To escape the typhoon. 逃離颱風
(B) To engage in recreational activities. 參加娛樂活動
(C) To go hiking in the mountains.
(D) To report on the storm.
報導暴風雨

＊sarcastic
a æ
諷刺的. 嘲月笑的. 挖苦的
He turned to me with a superior and sarcastic smile.
臉上露出傲慢的嘲笑微笑

＊offensive 討人厭的
廣告令女士們反感. 令人作嘔的
→ The advertisements were highly offensive to woman.

＊despite 不管. 任憑. 儘管
He went to work despite his illness.
Despite advanced years, she is learning to drive.
儘管年事已高. 她還在學開車

＊call in
對~表示懷疑 His honesty was called in question.
使起作用. 使行動起來 We'll call the new policy into action. 將實行新政策
使成立. 使產生: The organization was called into existence in 1985. 成立於1985
發揮. 調動 We should now call all positive factors into full play.
充分利用一切有利因素

＊mockery
嘲笑. 嘲弄. 笑柄. 假冒. 徒勞無功
Their mockery of Tom hurt his feeling.
His trial was a mockery of justice.
All our efforts were mockeries.

＊literally 逐字地. 照字面地
實在地. 不誇張地
The city was literally destroyed.
這城市真的被毀=滅了

GO ON TO THE NEXT PAGE.

*municipal 市的，市立的 He is in charge of the municipal housing project.
市辦的　　　　　　　　　　他主管這市的住房計畫

Ridgewood to Get New City Park
Feb. 15, 2020

*except for 除了~以外　The composition is quite good except for the spelling. 這篇文章除了拼字
都不錯

市議會成員昨晚會議同意新的市立公園的資金
City council members approved funds for a new municipal park at last
公園建設資金是從城市中所有購買中的銷售稅提出
night's meeting. Funds for the park's construction will come from a penny
除了食物和藥物
sales tax on all purchases made in the city, except for food and medicine.
公園預計畫在OL區　　　　　　　不令人意外的是
The park is planned for the Oak Leaf district. Unsurprisingly, there was
有些反對意見，來自其他區域的繳稅居民　　　　可是
some objection to the new tax from residents of other districts. However,
Baker 市長　　　保證他們　　　未來有改進案(建設)
Mayor Baker has assured citizens that future improvement projects are in
也會為了其他區域進行。
the works for other city districts.

*assure v. 擔保，使確信，使放心　→ 我向你保證這消息可靠
I can assure you of the reliability of the information.
Her future was assured, 她的未來是有保障的

Dear Mayor Baker,
reside 居　我是OL的居民，也就是新公園最近開幕的地方
I am a resident of Oak Leaf, where the new park was recently opened.
雖然我很欣賞你為了改善我們城市的這等做努力　我也希望
While I applaud your efforts to improve the environment of our city, I would
使你第一些 這個公園非預期中的影響(結果，後果)
like to make you aware of some unintended consequences of this new park.
我們都很感激有塊綠地可以享受　　　但是公園吸引
We all appreciate having a green area to enjoy, but the park has drawn
訪客從城市各地來　　　當然 每位市民都有權來享受
visitors from all over the city. Of course, every citizen has the right to enjoy
但停車在這區域已經變成真正的問題　　　車子常
the park, but parking has become a real problem in the area. Cars are often
是非法停在 鄰近區域　　並且引起附近居民很多不方便
illegally parked around the neighborhood and they cause a lot of
除此之外　　　　　很多的拜訪客
inconvenience for the residents. In addition to that, many of these visitors
帶來噪音和留下垃圾　　　當公園初開幕時
bring noise and leave their trash behind. When the park first opened, it was
是個放鬆的好地方　　現在常常有紙或其它垃圾留信
a beautiful place to relax. Now it is often littered with paper and other trash.
希望你可以處理這些問題，所以我們可以全部一起享受這個公園
I hope that you can address these problems so that we can all enjoy
Ridgewood's parks. *applaud v. 向~鼓掌 向~喝采
稱讚，贊成 We applauded him for his courage.
Sincerely, *consequence
Joe Smith n. 結果，後果 I'm willing to accept the consequence.
重大，重要 He is a man of great consequence 是個重要人物

*litter v. 弄得亂七八糟，充滿：The fire-place was littered with cigarette
n. 廢棄物，雜亂 Her room was in such a litter.　butts.

*behavior 行为举止、态度
→ He was on his best behavior. 他表现极好

Oak Leaf Park
Rules and Regulations 规定和规则

1. Park hours: 7AM – 10PM →公园边的街道不可停车
2. No parking on streets bordering the park. Please use the lot at Green St. and Long Brook Road. 不可乱丢垃圾
3. No littering. Please use the provided trash bins.
4. All dogs must be on a leash. → 所有狗要拴好 请使用提供的垃圾桶
5. No loud music at any time. 任何时候都不能有大声音乐
6. No fires. 不能开火

谢谢您的合作 cooperate v. 合作, 协作 +with
Thank you for your cooperation. n. ˊ ˇ j 合作社

*accidental adj.
偶然的, 意外的 Breaking the vase was purely accidental.
非主要的, 附属的, 附带的 accidental benefits 附带优惠   address v. 对~发话
卡 附带损失 collateral damage   →向~提出, 对付

186. Why did Joe Smith write the letter?
C
(A) To express his appreciation for the park. 表达对公园的感谢
(B) To suggest some rules for the park 建议一些规范
(C) To complain about some behaviors in the park. 抱怨公园里的一些行为
抗议 (D) To protest the increase in the sales tax. 抗议销售税的增加 →她坚决声明不曾做过那事
对 She protested that she had never done it. 曾做过那事

187. Why do people from other areas of the city visit Oak Leaf Park? 他们有付钱做建设
C
(A) They paid for its construction. 没有其他公园 build
(B) There are no other parks in the city.
(C) It is an attractive park. 是座吸引人的好公园 B
(D) In order to dump their trash.
为了丢垃圾 v. 倾倒, 抛弃, 倒垃圾 You'll be

188. Which of the following is closest in fined if you meaning to the phrase "unintended dump here.
A consequences"? result / effect / conclusion
(A) Unexpected outcomes 非预期的结果
(B) Accidental damage. 意外的伤害
(C) Unfair penalties. 不公平的惩罚
(D) Impolite behavior. 不礼貌的行为

189. What does Joe Smith mean when he says "address these problems"?
D
(A) The mayor should allow only people living in Oak Leaf to use the park. 市长应让住在这的人使用
(B) The mayor should make a speech about the problem. 应针对问题演讲
(C) The mayor should reply to Joe's letter. 应回信
(D) The mayor should do something about the problems. 应做些事

regulate v. 管理, 控制, 调节
190. How many of the regulations are related to the problems that Joe Smith mentioned?
(A) Two. 现在对喝酒
(B) Three. 2、3、5 开车的人
(C) Five. 处罚更严了
(D) Six. ①

* penalty n. 处罚, 刑罚 ↑
There are now stiffer penalties for drunken drivers.
回行为造成的 不利结果. 损失, 苦难
They had to pay the penalties for telling the lie.

GO ON TO THE NEXT PAGE.

Questions 191-195 refer to the following form and two e-mails.

IAAC 2020 Online Registration	
* indicates required field. 指示.指出.表明.象徵.暗示	
Name* *organize v. 組織.安排	His hesitation indicates unwillingness.
Organization We'll organize an event.	他的猶豫表明不願意
Address 使有條理.使井然有序	Please indicate to the organizers
E-mail* The story is well organized.	where you would like to sit.
Phone Number 這個故事結構嚴謹	請向組織者(主辦者)說明你想坐哪
Have you attended IAAC before?	☐ Yes ☐ No 兒
I will attend* *register v. 註冊.登記 申報.流露 Her face registered surprise. 登記.註冊.掛号 臉上露出驚訝之色	☐ October 15 掛号 I want the letter registered. ☐ October 16 ☐ October 17 我想掛号寄達封信
Registration Fee* gun voter land] registration 槍枝 選民 登記 土地	☐ Single-day registration $75.00 ☐ Two-day registration $125.00 ☐ Three-day registration $160.00

*itinerary 留下行程.以防緊急
[aɪˈtɪnəˌrɛrɪ] 時刻要找你

To:	registration@IAAC.org [aɪˈtɪnəˌrɛrɪ]
From:	jmcdaniels@ucanberra.edu n. 旅程.旅行計畫(記錄)
Subject:	Registration questions Leave your itinerary so that we
Date:	July 1, 2020 (款) can reach you in case of emergency.

我寫这封信想詢問你們的退貨政策   我計畫參加
I am writing this e-mail to inquire about your refund policy. I plan to
行会議
attend two days of the conference, October 16-October 17. However,
可是会議還沒如此久遠   对我來說很難100%確定我的旅遊行
with the conference so far off, it is difficult for me to be 100 percent sure
我目前安排去馬德里是 10/15   程
of my travel itinerary. I am currently scheduled to arrive in Madrid on
但我可能   晚到一天   因此 我可能錯过
October 15, but I may be delayed by one day. Therefore, I may miss the
第二天の会   那样の話   我有可能得到註冊2日活动的部分退款嗎?
second day. In that case, would I be entitled to a partial refund of my
two-day registration? I would appreciate a speedy response as I know
the conference tickets are in high demand. 若你儘快回覆我會很感謝
*transfer   市場需求大 因為我知道会議の票售很快
Sincerely, v. 搬.調動.轉換 Her father transferred her to a better school.
James McDaniels, Ph.D. 轉讓 To preserve the farm intact, adj. 完整無缺の
University of Canberra he transferred it to one heir. 為了保持農場の完整

他特意轉交給一個繼承人 [ɛr] 繼承人

To:	jmcdaniels@ucanberra.edu
From:	lprescott@IAAC.org
Subject:	Registration questions
Date:	July 2, 2020

*flexibility n. 彈性.易曲性.適應性
We appreciate your flexibility in dealing with this matter.

Dear Dr. McDaniels,

the flexibility of the wire 線的彈性
plastic 塑料的彈性

謝你對於參加会議的兴趣，也謝你的提問

Thank you for your interest in the conference and for your
question. You are correct in thinking that the tickets are in high
你覺得票張快就賣完是没錯的
demand. Therefore, I would like to explain your options so that
因此   我想和你解釋你的選擇
you can make your decision as soon as possible.
所以你可以盡快做決定

如同我們網站說的   所有会議的票都是不可退款的
As stated on our website, all conference tickets are
也不可轉讓的   因此   若你購買
non-refundable and non-transferrable. Therefore, if you purchase
一張2日票而只能參加一天
a two-day registration and are able to attend only one day, you
你將無法對於没使用到的部分退款
will not be eligible for a refund of the unused portion. You could
你可以單買10/17 一日票
purchase only a single-day registration for October 17. That
那樣会給你彈性 若你10/16有空再買另張 單日票
would give you the flexibility to purchase another single-day
能夠   可是
ticket for October 16 if you are able to attend. However, there is
有很大的機会那天可能会   没票
a good chance that there may be no tickets available on that day.
我給你的建議   若財允許   就買2日票
My advice to you, if finances allow, is to go ahead and purchase
為了確保你能參加 所有你提參加的活
the two-day registration in order to ensure that you can attend all 动
of the activities you wish.

還有我能幫上忙的地方,請不要猶豫.聯繫我
If I can be of any further assistance, please do not hesitate
to contact me. *eligible adj. 法律上合格的.有资格当選的
out law
He is eligible for retirement. 合乎退休條件
Sincerely,
②合適的.合意的: She married to an eligible bachelor.
嫁给了中意的單身汉
Lee Prescott *flexible adj. 可彎曲的.有彈性的.柔順的.可變通的 (4)

→ We need a foreign policy that is more flexible.

GO ON TO THE NEXT PAGE.

191. What will happen in Madrid on October 15, 2020?

~~gun~~ voter registration 核查 選民 登記

(A) James McDaniels will arrive in Madrid. register n.v. 註冊 登記

(B) Registration for the IAAC will be completed. IAAC活動註冊完成

(C) An international conference will begin. 國際會議開始

→ v. 確認. 確定

(D) Mr. McDaniels will confirm the dates that he will attend the IAAC. 確認日期

The queen confirmed the treaty. 批准此項條約

192. What problem does James McDaniels have? 拖欠. 給予. 買得起. 有足夠的

(A) He cannot attend the conference.

(B) He cannot afford to pay the three-day registration fee. 付不起這三的費用

deny 否定 否認 (C) He was denied a discount on the registration fee. 他被拒絕註冊費打折

(D) He does not know exactly when he will arrive in Madrid. 他不知道要選何時到

193. If Dr. McDaniels registers for two days, but attends only one, how much will he pay?

(A) $75.

(B) $150.

(C) $125.

(D) $50.

* Transfer

She has been transferred to another department.

At the port, the goods were transferred onto the ship.

Within a few years they had transferred barren wastes into firtile fields.

You transfer the embroidery design from the paper to cloth by pressing it with a warm iron.

To preserve the farm intact, he transferred it to one heir.

adj. 完整無缺的. 未受損傷的

The delicate package arrived intact.

transferable 可轉移的

transform 使改變. 改善. The situation has been greatly transformed.

194. Which of the following must be filled in on the form in order to register for the conference? 為了註冊會議下面何者需填上

(A) The name of the organization one represents. 參加人代表的組織名稱

(B) A phone number where one can be contacted. 可聯絡到的号碼

(C) The dates that one wishes to attend. 想參加的日期

(D) One's previous experience with IAAC conferences. 之前參加過的 經驗

195. Why does Lee Prescott advise Dr. McDaniels to register for two days?

(A) Day two of the conference is the most important day.

(B) All registration fees are non-refundable. 不可退款的

(C) There is a limit to the number of tickets available. 有效票有限

(D) Day two of the conference is already sold out. 第二天的票已賣完

adj. 可利用的, 可得到的, 可買到的, 有空的

→ The principle is available now.

42

Dear Parents,

Spring is here, and it is time to start planning our annual Crafts Fair. As you know, the proceeds of the fair will go toward funding interesting field trips and outings for children in grades 4 through 6. The fair will be Saturday, April 25, so there is still lots of time to create some projects for sale. We're looking for any hand-made item, from pots to banana bread. If you're not the crafty type, don't worry. There are lots of other ways you can help make the fair a success. We'll be holding our first organizational meeting next Thursday at 4:00 in room 303.

Come out and support our school!

Melanie Carter

PTA president

My son / daughter _____ in _____
                        (child's name)   (teacher's name)
class has my permission to attend the school field trip on May 10.

I understand that I should pick up my child from school no later than 4pm on May 10.

☐ I am available to attend this field trip as a chaperone.

☐ I am not available to attend this field trip as a chaperone.

Parent's signature: _____ Date: _____

GO ON TO THE NEXT PAGE.

43

*appreciate v. 欣賞, 感激, 感謝, 體會, 增值　　她的音樂才能沒人賞識

Dear Ms. Albertson, Her talent for music was not appreciated.

謝謝你帶我和班上同學們參觀你的博物館
Thank you for showing me and my classmates your museum
我玩得很 開心　　也學到很多
yesterday. I had a really good time, and I learned a lot. I liked the
我最喜歡鯊魚展覽　　又大又酷
shark exhibit the most. They were really big and cool. I'm going
我要去研究更多鯊魚資訊的事　　我想成為一位海洋科學家
to study more about sharks. I want to be an ocean scientist when I
grow up. Maybe I can help the sharks and the other sea creatures.
當我長大時.　　也許我能幫助鯊魚和其他海洋生物

Sincerely, → I'm afraid you have not appreciated the
Billy Taylor   urgency of the matter. 恐怕你尚未意識到這件事的急迫性

→ Land will continue to appreciate. 土地將繼續增值

*appreciation   增值 → Her appreciation of Amy's chances of getting
n. 欣賞, 鑑賞, 賞識, 感謝   the promotion was correct. 他對Amy晉升机会的估計是對

196. When was Melanie's letter most likely
B written?　　　*craft
(A) April 25.　　n. 工艺, 手艺.
(B) March 15.　　→ He learned his craft from an
(C) May 10.　　old master
(D) May 1.
　　n. 行业, 职业 → He learned the mason's
197. Where did the students most likely go craft.
D on May 10?　　他學水泥匠這一行.
(A) The zoo.
(B) An art museum.　crafty① 喜做手工艺品的
(C) A water park.　②adj. 狡猾的, 詭計多端的
(D) A natural science museum.
　　　　a crafty politician
　　　　老奸巨猾的政客

198. Why did Billy Taylor write his letter?
B (A) To ask for a scholarship. 要求獎學金
　　　　　　　　up
(A) (B) To express appreciation. 表達感謝
(C) To arrange a visit. 安排拜訪
(D) To submit his homework.
under | send 繳交作業
v. 繳交, 呈送, 使服從　　　聽從法庭裁決
We'll submit ourselves to the court's judgements.

199. What does Melanie Carter mean by 的
D "not the crafty type"?
(A) Honest. 誠實
(B) Not very intelligent. 不太聰明
(C) Not interested in art. 對藝術沒興趣
(D) Not good at making things.
　　不太會做東西　　監護人
200. What does the word "chaperone" as
A used in the form most likely mean?
(A) Supervisor.　/ˈʃæp.ə.roʊn/
(B) Driver.　= chaperon
(C) Teacher.
(D) Parent.
　　　　*intelligent
　　adj. 有才智的, 聰明的

→ The child made a very
　　intelligent comment.

→ Elephants are intelligent animals.
　　有靈性的動物

→ He has been very intelligent about
　the whole thing. 他對全程很了解.

Stop! This is the end of the test. If you finish before time is called, you may go
back to Parts 5, 6, and 7 and check your work.

44